A HIGHER AUTHORITY

Published In 2023 By Carol Bissett

© Copyright Carol Bissett

Book and Cover design by Russell Holden
www.pixeltweakspublications.com

All rights reserved without limiting the rights under copyright reserved above, no parts of this publication may be preproduced, stored in or introduced into a retrieval system, or transmitted in any form, or by any means (electronic, mechanical, photocopying, recording or otherwise) without the prior written permission of both the copyright owner and the publisher of this book.

ACKNOWLEDGMENTS

Firstly I would like to thank all the people who have helped me to get this book published.
To Liz, my wonderful editor, who points out all the issues involved in killing people, and pulls me back from the brink. But only in my stories, of course.
To Russ Holden of Pixel Tweaks Publications, for another stunning book cover.
To my son and IT guru, Jon, for all the help he gives me without laughing at my inaptitude, and for uploading my manuscripts so I have both e-books and paperbacks to sell.
To my Beta readers, Ann, Josh, Sofie, Mark and Julie. Their feedback and honesty, but kind suggestions can only make my book a better read.
To Rise Cinema for my trailer. It was a blast guys, and thank you.
Also to The Temple Church, Fleet Street, London, EC4Y 7HL. A hidden treasure, which I can highly recommend to you next time you are in London.
I would like to take this chance to thank the staff at The Temple Church for all their help with my research.
For my characters, I do use some of the titles that are still used within The Temple Church, with a few adaptions. However, the storyline is totally fiction, and has no bearing to any persons, past or present, and any likeness is purely coincidental.

And lastly to all my loyal readers. Thank you for your patience. This book took longer to publish than I had promised it would, and I hope the wait was worth it.

DEDICATION

To Dan, Sara, Ben and Jon.
You are my world

THE PROLOGUE

Lost to the mists of time, a document of a story that could be so cataclysmic, that it could rock the foundations of what we have been led to believe.

But does this document still exist? Did it ever exist? Or is the whole thing a lie?

The Knights Templar, guardians of holy relics, were entrusted with this most sacred article, or so it is believed.

Now, in our modern world, rumor is rife that the artifact does indeed still exist, and this possibility is making some groups very nervous, so much so, people are dying, or are these deaths just a terrible coincidence?

A story of myth, legend and conspiracy travels across the sea, and lands firmly in the lap of The Cheshire Serious Crime Squad.

THE WARRINGTON DETECTIVE

A Higher Authority

CHAPTER ONE

Detective Inspector Cassie Rowden looked at the body and wondered yet again, how one human could inflict such horror on another. It didn't make her sad or depressed, just thoughtful.

She shivered, and even though it was before seven a.m., it was already a warm August morning, so her reaction was nothing to do with being cold.

'What do you think?'

Cassie jumped at the sound; she was so deep in thought. Dr John Baron was standing next to her, and the setting they were in made his ghostlike appearance seem almost normal. 'Good morning to you as well John.' She smiled as he grunted at her.

'Ritualistic. Got to be,' he commented.

'What gave it away?' asked Cassie. 'The cross burnt into his chest, or the fact he's been nailed to a plank of wood?' The man's arms were spread as far apart as they could be, secured by a large nail in each palm, it was brutal and Cassie had to look away.

'I was thinking more of this.' He held up a large evidence bag with dark cloth inside.

Cassie frowned. 'What's that?'

'A black shirt, a black jacket and a dog collar,' John said. 'Found at the altar.'

'So he was a priest?' Cassie said quietly.

'Dressed as one, at the very least.'

They stood for a moment, contemplative. Then Cassie broke the sacred silence. 'Anything else?'

'Blood, lots of blood, but nothing else yet. And before you ask, I don't know the time of death. What I can say is that it was after eleven pm and he was found at six this morning by a jogger.'

'Makes a change from a dog walker anyhow. Probably he died between eleven and...?'

'He's been dead at least six hours, according to his body

temperature, and that's all I'm saying until I get him on the table.'

'Curious. I wonder what the DCI would have made of this?' Cassie said, almost to herself.

'Do you miss her?' John asked, as quietly.

'Yes. Do you?'

'Every day.'

***

Professor Johan threw a few things into his small case. He had a plane to catch, and if he didn't get a move on, he'd miss his flight. Still, John Lennon Airport was only a short car journey from his house at Sefton Park on the outskirts of Liverpool.

He was flying to Malta. A colleague had emailed him about a lead they were both following, and time was running out. If he didn't get to the artefact quickly it would disappear, probably for another couple of hundred years.

'Passport, where did I put my passport?' he asked himself out loud. 'My desk?' He opened the drawer and tossed papers around, then saw it sitting on top of the desk where he had put it last night. 'Ah, yes.' He clutched it to his body, closed his eyes, and took a deep breath before putting it into his jacket pocket.

The doorbell rang and the professor looked at his watch. 'Taxi's early' he said to himself.' Never mind.' He went to answer the door. 'Sorry, can you wait, please?' I won't be—'

Those were the last words the professor ever uttered as a twelve-inch stiletto blade was expertly pushed into his chest. It perforated the left ventricle, and as it was twisted clockwise the left atrium was incised as well.

Professor Johan was dead before he hit the ground.

***

Wen pushed her crying daughter in her pram, hoping the walk would do its usual magic and send her to sleep. This was the third day that Daisy had been fretful, and the third night that Wen hadn't had much rest.

After ten minutes or so the babies' cries became less frequent and quieter, until finally the leafy, wealthy lanes of Appleton became peaceful once again. Wen sighed and looked at her infant daughter as she continued to walk, afraid that lack of motion would wake her. 'It's a good job you're beautiful,' she said quietly, 'because you're not very nice to be around at the moment.'

Doctors and health visitors had all reassured Wen that Daisy was well, but suffering from colic, and as this coincided with Wen giving up breastfeeding, she could see the logic in their explanations. But she had never really been on board with the whole earth-mother thing, especially as she had been heavily sedated for the first three days after Daisy's birth. This had been by caesarean section, four weeks early.

Her last memory before the birth was the sight of Jeff, Daisy's father, being gunned down as someone tried to strangle her. She was saved by a coach of day trippers, on their way to Liverpool, who came across the horrific scene just in time – for Wen, at least. Unsurprisingly, maternal bonding hadn't really happened.

Wen had never felt that pull of overpowering love which she had read other mothers felt from the moment they set eyes on their baby. She felt protective, she felt responsible for Daisy, but unconditional love?

Her phone vibrated in her pocket. It was permanently on silent these days, since it had woken Daisy on more than one occasion. Wen's wardrobe was now restricted to items with pockets.

Wen pulled out the phone. She expected the call to be from Aran, her twin brother. He needed to know where she and the baby were at all times, requiring constant reassurance that they were both safe. However, it was not Aran.

'Hello, sir,' said Wen.

'Wen. How are you?'

'Good, sir. Just out for a walk with the baby.'

'Yes, good. Excellent, and how is little...'
'Daisy.'
'Yes, Daisy.'
'Fine, sir.'
'Good. Excellent.' There was a pause.

'Can I help you, sir?' As much as she would like to think that her chief inspector was ringing solely to enquire after her health and that of her baby, she knew from experience that he wanted something.

'I'm hoping so, Wen. I do realise that you still have quite a lot of leave to take, but...'

'But?'

'You'll see it on the news later, so I thought I should let you know beforehand. The professor you dealt with over that artefact...'

'Professor Johan?'

'Yes, that's the chap. He died this morning, in his flat. Murdered.'

Wen stopped dead and sat on a low wall. 'Murdered?'

'Yes, and that's not all. He was on his way to Malta. He had a lead on something to do with that book; a colleague said he thought he knew where it was. The colleague was also found dead this morning, killed in much the same way. The Malta police rang the last number on their murder victim's phone and it was answered by Liverpool Murder Squad. They were at their crime scene when they picked up the call.'

'Connected then?'

'Bit too much of a coincidence, don't you think?'

'Yes sir, I do.'

'And there's more. A body was found this morning at Norton Priory. We aren't sure yet, but that may also be linked. That's why I'd like you to come in, if you feel you can.'

'What? Back to work, now?'

'Only if you can. Just a session a week, maybe, as a consultant for the team? Name your own hours.' He sounded desperate.

'I'll have to sort out childcare,' said Wen, her mind racing.

'Of course, of course. I quite—'
'Is tomorrow soon enough?'

CHAPTER TWO

'You want to do *what?*'

Aran turned away from his cheese sauce, waving a wooden spoon wildly at his sister, and she wondered if death by sticky spoon had ever been a thing.

'I said I'd pop in tomorrow, just for a few hours,' Wen said, hoping her voice carried the authority she was aiming for, but fearing it sounded more apologetic than anything else.

'But – but what about Daisy?' The spoon got nearer to Wen's face. She couldn't remember ever seeing her brother so angry. Aran was usually mild mannered, to the point of seeming not to care much about anything. He did get upset, just like neurotypical people, but not often.

'I'll take her with me,' said Wen, with a shrug.

'*What?* There are germs and viruses everywhere, and she's only had one set of vaccinations!'

Wen had to step back at this point. She was very tempted to tell Aran to drop the spoon, or else.

'I thought the plan was to interview nannies in a few weeks and go back when she was six months old?'

'Aran, I'm not going back to work as such. I'm providing input on a very tricky case. I can come and go as I please, and when they're on the right track, I'll pick up my maternity leave again. In fact, I'll be at home longer than planned.'

Her brother opened his mouth to say something else, but a strong smell of burning made them both look at the stove. Aran ran across to see what the damage was. 'Now look what you made me do!' he cried, seizing the pan. 'That's ruined. I'll have to start again.'

He put the pan in the sink and started running water onto the glutinous mess. The hissing steam rising from the offending object was even more choking than the smell of burning cheese.

Then he turned back to his sister. 'Why?'

'Why what?' she said, stalling for time.

Aran folded his arms and waited.

Wen sighed. 'Do you remember the professor who wanted The Book?'

'Professor Johan?'

'Yes. He was murdered this morning. The Chief wants my input as I've been in contact with him since...' She gathered herself. 'Since it was stolen.'

'Oh.'

'It might lead to the murdering bastards who killed Jeff.'

Aran frowned. 'And it might affect you. In a bad way, I mean.'

'Don't worry, Aran.' Wen knew that her brother was, quite rightly, concerned that she might not be able to cope with work linked to Jeff's murder. However, she felt it would be very therapeutic to play a role in catching his killers.

Her sleeping daughter, who was tucked up in her pram in the porch, had not been planned. In fact, she was a small miracle. Wen had undergone medical treatment for a serious gynaecological condition, and had been told that she would never have children. Confirmation of her pregnancy was therefore both a shock and a thrill for the parents-to-be.

The plan had been for Wen to take a year off after the birth. When she went back to work, Jeff would take a twelve-month sabbatical from the university where he lectured on criminal psychology and write another book. This meant their child wouldn't start nursery until she was two, which both Jeff and Wen thought was a good time for her to start mixing with other tots.

That had been the plan. It hadn't allowed for Jeff being murdered, Wen being half-strangled and Daisy appearing four weeks early.

Because Wen had been heavily sedated for seventy-two hours after delivery, she hadn't been very receptive to what was required to fulfil the needs of a tiny baby. Once out of hospital she managed, just about, to get through each day. This was thanks mostly to her brother, who took over a lot of the baby's care. Daisy seemed to bond with her uncle from the get-go, and she was much calmer when he was around.

But Aran had always said that he wasn't going to be a full-time childminder if – no, when – his sister went back to work.

Now Aran stood, thinking. 'OK, I'll look after her,' he said at last.

'Thank you.'

'But just for a few hours a day, over the next few weeks. Deal?'

'Deal.'

'Now I have to start my cheese sauce all over again, and you owe me a new pan.'

Aran went back to his cooking. There were things he did, and things he never did. For example, a lady cleaned for them three times a week, but she was forbidden to enter Aran's rooms.

He also hardly ever went out. That was one of the reasons why he wouldn't – couldn't – look after Daisy for more than a few hours at a time. Her needs might force him from his home, the only place where he felt safe.

Wen watched him cook; his back turned. She knew just how much it would cost her brother to babysit for her, and for that she was grateful. There wasn't a soul on this planet that she trusted more to care for her daughter.

CHAPTER THREE

Cassie Rowden stood in the office of the Cheshire Serious Crime Squad and contemplated the murder board, tapping a pen on her teeth. On the board were a few names and locations, some crime-scene photos, and sod all else.

Her team waited. As usual, the quiet murmur which had greeted her as she entered the large team room had become a loud rumbling.

'OK,' she said. The volume didn't alter. *'Everyone listen up!'* Her team parked their conversations, to be continued later.

'As you all know, this body '– she pointed to the photo of the dead man at Norton Priory, 'was found early yesterday morning. Dr Baron's immediate findings are that he died from hypovolemic shock: in other words, blood loss. This man had been tortured. His nails were pulled out, the soles of his feet were beaten and he also sustained brutal injuries from this vicious assault. That's before someone burnt a cross on his chest and nailed his hands to a plank of wood. Both these things, Dr Baron thinks, happened before his death.' Even the more hardened members of Cassie's staff looked disgusted and horrified.

'We found some items of clothing which we suspect belonged to the victim, and these may indicate that he was a priest.' She pointed to a photo of the clothes. 'What we don't know yet is who he is. No one has been reported missing from any of the local churches, and DC Wall spent yesterday phoning around the area, but all their priests and vicars were accounted for.'

She faced her team. 'So, who is he? Where did he come from, and why was he killed in this way?'

'Kiddie fiddler? Someone getting their revenge is my bet,' said a voice at the back. It was Peter Blake, one of her younger, very enthusiastic new officers.

'Thank you, DC Blake. I think we can put it more succinctly

than that.' She turned back to the board and wrote *Possible paedophile.* 'Any other ideas?'

'It might be a bit more complicated than that.' This voice came from the doorway, and belonged to Wen Price. Cassie didn't know whether to run over and hug her or say what she was thinking, which was *What the hell are you doing here?*

As Wen walked into the room someone started to clap. This quickly spread, and soon the whole team were on their feet, applauding. Wen blushed, and nodded at the team with a small, quiet 'Thank you.'

Cassie quickly escorted her boss into the office and shut the door. She automatically moved behind the desk, then stopped. 'Do you want to...?' She pointed at the chair.

'Hell, no. It's your office now.' Wen wanted to add 'For now,' but didn't. Normally, the DI & DCI each had their own offices. However, Wen had stayed in her old office when promoted, rather than move along the corridor to her predecessor's room. She liked to be near the action, and that wouldn't change when she returned to her post, whenever that was. She sat down on the other side of the desk, putting down her bag and slipping off her coat.

'You're not back from leave yet, are you?' asked Cassie, in a tone filled with concern both for her boss and her own position in the squad.

'No. I'm just here to give you the benefit of my insight into this investigation, if I can. The Chief called me yesterday and asked me to give you a few hours here and there, because of my connection with the case.'

'What connection?' Cassie felt thoroughly confused.

'He hasn't spoken to you yet.' This was a statement, not a question. 'I'll bring you up to date, as far as I can.' Wen summarised what she knew.

'But how did they get a link from our body to the prof?'

'Not sure yet, but the Zoom meeting should answer some of our questions. I received a call last night from a DCI Wild, part of Liverpool Murder Team. He is the SIO for the professor's murder and he wants to speak to you today, with me on the call.'

Cassie bristled at not having been informed about this first, but tried not to show it.

'I know what you're thinking,' said Wen. 'You're annoyed that you weren't told. And yes, I'd be fuming if I were in your shoes. However, they still aren't sure about this possible link, and DCI Wild wanted more background on Professor Johan before he spoke to you.'

'You kept in touch with the professor, then?'

'I had no choice. He even came to see me in hospital. He asked me what happened, did I see anyone, what were they wearing. Luckily, a nurse threw him out. I was very stressed by it.'

'I'm not bloody surprised. What on earth was he thinking?'

'He phoned me a week later to apologise, stressing how important The Book is, and that the police had to find it. I pointed out that I was more interested in finding out who had killed Jeff. Then he told me that he couldn't sleep at night for thinking about it all, because if we hadn't been taking the book to him, none of it would have happened. Anyway, after that he called me most weeks to see how Daisy and I were getting on. I wouldn't say we became good friends, exactly, but we were more than acquaintances.'

'Right. 'Cassie considered this.' I had no idea. I should have visited you more, Wen. I'm sorry. But you know what this job does to you.'

Wen smiled.'It's OK, Cassie. To be honest, I didn't want people visiting: I was too wrapped up in my own pain. I think that coming in a few hours a week to help with this case will actually do me good, to be honest.'

'Maybe. Anyway, how's Daisy? Who's looking after her today?'

'Aran.'

'*Aran?*'

'Yep. He's fantastic with her, but only for short periods. I'll sort out a nanny or a nursery before I come back full-time, but he's offered to help for this case. He was horrified when I said I'd bring her with me. Apparently, you're all germ-ridden.' Wen laughed.

Cassie smiled, then put her work face back on. 'What time is this Zoom call arranged for, then?'

Wen looked at her watch. 'Wen. We've just time for a coffee before it starts.'

At exactly ten am the Zoom meeting started, with introductions all round. A detective from Malta was also on the call, which neither of the women were expecting. Detective Luca Vella was in his mid-thirties, very dark and extremely good looking, whereas DCI Brendan Wild was overweight, balding, and probably close to retirement age.

'Thank you for your time, everyone,' said Wild.' Hopefully, we can get a more coherent view of what has been going on with these three murder victims, and ascertain if they are indeed connected.'

'Well, we have little doubt that the murder of Professor Johan and Dr Dolenz are connected, 'said the Maltese detective. 'They were ex-colleagues and friends, and both had a passion for religious artefacts. In fact, Carlo Dolenz was known locally as the Holy Grail Hunter.'

'Really? 'said Cassie, with a smile.' Now that I've heard of.'

'It was an affectionate nickname, DI Rowden, but he was always off here and there on his quests.' Luca made it all sound very romantic and rather like Tomb Raider. 'He teaches – taught – Latin at the university here. A part-time job, I understand, to help with his pension from the UK.'

'Just Cassie, please,' she replied, with a flutter of her eyelashes, and Luca smiled.

'Please carry on with your hypothesis, Detective Vella,' interjected Wen, giving Cassie rather a stern glance off-camera.

'Dr Dolenz was due to pick up Professor Johan from the airport: it was in his diary. We have accessed his computer and read recent emails. Both the doctor and the professor were concerned for their safety, especially after what happened to you, DCI Price. And may I say at this point that I am very sorry for your loss.'

Wen nodded without speaking.

DCI Wild cleared his throat. 'Did Dr Dolenz think he'd found this Book of...' He paused and consulted something to the side of his screen.' Book of Sceleratis?'

'Ah, that we don't know,' said Luca Vella. 'However, after looking at his emails, I suspect this was a clue to where the actual artefact was. As we know, the one you found in Warrington was a copy of the original. I will send you both copies of these files, but there was little else of interest. I've left it with Digital to see if they can find anything more.'

The others nodded their thanks, and Luca continued.' As they were both killed at the same time, with the same type of weapon, it leaves little doubt that their murders were coordinated and connected.'

'As for our murdered priest,' said DCI Wild, 'we have a CCTV shot of him with the professor from two days ago. They were in the café at the World Museum in Liverpool. We still don't know who he was, or their connection, but by the manner of his death, he must have had some information that somebody wanted really badly.'

'The whereabouts of The Book?' asked Cassie.

'Possibly,' replied DCI Wild.' It's more likely that he knew what the professor and the doctor had uncovered, which was why—'

'Why he was killed so quickly,' said Wen. 'No need to torture him, because the killers already had the information.'

'Anyway,' said Luca, 'whoever took The Book at the ambush that saw your partner killed would still have it, surely?'

'You would think so,' answered the Liverpool detective. 'Unless those people stole it because of its intrinsic value, with the view that they could sell it.'

Wen shook her head slowly.' I don't think treasure hunters would try to murder two people in broad daylight. It felt darker than that.' A shiver ran up her spine as she tried to shut out the vision of Jeff's head exploding at point-blank range.

'But who would go to such lengths, and why?' asked Cassie.

'This was very well orchestrated. Very professional.'

'Now that is the question, Cassie,' said Luca. 'We do have some ideas on that, but at the moment that is all they are: ideas.'

'Come on then, don't keep it to yourself. Share, please,' Cassie said, with a broad smile.

'OK, but it's a bit out there. The Knights Templar.'

'What?' said Wen.

'The professor went on about them when he came to look at The Book. But surely, they don't exist any more? They've been gone for hundreds of years,' said Cassie, almost laughing at this ridiculous idea.

'That's what they want you to believe,' said Luca, with a smile.

CHAPTER FOUR

The meeting closed with a to-do list for all parties. Cassie would go to Liverpool tomorrow to work with DCI Wild, questioning some of the professor's close contacts as well as people who claimed to have seen the professor with the priest.

Luca would make discreet enquiries about the Knights Templar in Malta. It wasn't't the first time the society's name had come up, he said, usually in connection with the church, but previous investigations had drawn a blank.

Wen would do some research at home on the possible existence of Knights Templar in the UK. They had scheduled another Zoom meeting in two days 'time.

'I'll task a couple of the team with checking arrivals from Malta over the past couple of days,' said Cassie. 'Both in Liverpool and Manchester, though that's presuming the professor's murderer came from Malta in the first place.'

'And also that if they did, they flew into one of those airports,' added Wen. She scratched her head.' Needle and haystack spring to mind.' The two women smiled at each other. 'Oh well, I'd better get back to my daughter and my brother,' said Wen, looking at her watch. 'What else are you working on just now Cassie?'

'We have an attempted murder coming to court before the end of the month,' Cassie replied. 'The rest of the team have enough to be getting on with.'

Wen got up and put her coat on.' See you in two days, then. Can you give me a bell each evening, please, Cassie, to update me?'

'Yes, no problem. I might even get a trip to Malta out of this. What do you reckon?'

'You'll be lucky, with all the budget cuts,' Wen said matter-of-factly.

'Pity,' said Cassie. 'Luca's very easy on the eye.'
Wen studied her colleague. 'I thought you were gay?'
Cassie just smiled.

***

'How did it go?' Aran asked, as soon as Wen walked through the door. He was in the kitchen, carefully folding a pile of Daisy's clothes fresh from the tumble dryer.

'Good,' Wen replied, as she sank into a chair and kicked off her shoes.

'Oh. I was hoping you would say it was an awful mistake and you had no intention of ever going back.' Aran said this without the slightest inflection in his voice. Was it a plea, was it irony, was it sarcasm?

'I'll be working from home, and I have to go back into the office in two days' time for a meeting. Just for a few hours.'

Aran stopped what he was doing and stayed perfectly still for about ten seconds, then nodded. 'OK. What time?'

'That's me done,' called Alice Guess, their cleaner. She came into the room, picked up Wen's shoes from the two different bits of floor where they had landed, tutted, and placed them neatly in a corner. 'How your parents could have twins who are so different I do not know. Bye, then.' She walked towards the door, took her coat from the rack and slipped it on before leaving.

Wen looked at her brother. 'What?' he said, with a shrug.

'Tell me again why we put up with Alice?'

'We? You mean why do you, the untidy person living in this house, put up with her? She is fine with me. She turns up on time, leaves me alone, and gets on with her work. I trust her.'

Wen couldn't argue with that. 'How's Daisy been?' she asked, to change the subject.

'Fine. She's asleep in her room.' He nodded towards the baby monitor as he folded a sleepsuit.

'Great. I'll get some work done while she's quiet.'

'And what work would that be?'

'Trying to trace descendants of the Knights Templar in the UK.'

'Good luck with that.'

'What? Don't you think there are any?' Wen sat at the kitchen table and opened her laptop.

'I'm sure there are, but I don't think you'll find them. If the professor couldn't, what makes you think you can?' Aran wasn't being scathing, as an outsider listening in might have thought: he was being realistic. It kept Wen's feet on the ground.

'He might have been very clever, Aran, but I'm a police officer. This is what I do, and I'm good at it.'

***

Cassie took the train to Liverpool the following day: a twenty to thirty-minute journey from Warrington. DCI Wild had said he would meet her at the station. He was as good as his word, standing at the end of the platform with a warm smile on his face. 'Welcome to Liverpool, DI Rowden,' he said as he shook her hand.

'Thank you, sir,' she said.' Good of you to pick me up.' Cassie had expected a uniformed officer to meet her and take her to the museum, where they had arranged to interview some of the staff and Professor Johan's colleagues. Afterwards, they would drive to the crime scene: Professor Johan's flat at Sefton Park.

'I thought we could interview people in the cafe,' said DCI Wild, as they walked towards the waiting car. 'Less formal to meet them at their place of work. Less intimidating. People are more likely to chat if we have a coffee and keep it light, don't you find?'

'Definitely,' replied Cassie. To be honest, she preferred the comfort of an interview room, even though that hadn't stopped a witness attacking her and putting her in the local intensive care unit for a few days not so long ago.

Within minutes, they were pulling into the back entrance of

a formidable building. As Cassie got out of the car, she looked in awe at the height and grandeur of it all. Inside did not disappoint, either. The facility, which looked from the outside as if it should belong in Rome, had such beautiful modern interior architecture that Cassie didn't know where to look. 'How did I not know about this place?' she said, as she tried to keep up with the DCI.

'It's fabulous, isn't it? A hidden gem, but it shouldn't be. It was opened in 1860 to replace the Derby Museum, but a lot of it had to be rebuilt after the war. It was badly damaged in the Blitz in 1941.'

He stopped suddenly and Cassie almost cannoned into him. 'Here we are,' he said, and opened a door for her, standing aside to allow her through.

'You know a lot about this place, 'she commented as she entered the café.

'I was an architect before I joined the force. What would you like to drink, tea or coffee?'

'Coffee, please. Flat white if they have it.'

'Right, I'll order. You go and sit down through there.' DCI Wild pointed to a door at the side of the café, through which Cassie could just see another room.

'We're going in there?'

'Yep. Hi, it's Susan, isn't it? Hi, love. Can we have a tea and a flat white coffee please, and we'll wait in there for you.'

Cassie entered the side room, which was dark. She felt inside the door for the light switches and flicked them on. Light cascaded into the room, revealing a large dining space with a huge glass chandelier suspended from the high ceiling. 'Oh my God! 'she exclaimed.

DCI Wild came through and switched off some of the lights. 'No need to burn too much electricity, Cassie. I can call you Cassie, can't I?'

'What? Oh yes, sir.' Cassie was still taking in her surroundings.

The lady who had taken their order entered with a tray. 'One tea, one flat white, and two freshly made scones, my treat.'

'Thank you, Susan. Come and sit with us.' DCI Wild undid his jacket, sat at a random table and pointed to the seat opposite him. Susan placed the tray on the table and sat down. 'Cassie?'

She realised he was asking her to join them. 'Yes. Sorry.' She sat down on the same side as the DCI and reached for her drink.

'I thought we could see people in here.' He nodded towards the woman who had provided them with refreshments. 'Susan, who is the café manager, has kindly agreed to let us use this room.'
She looked in her mid-fifties, tall, with cropped hair and bright-blue eyes. 'We only use it at busy times, during the school holidays, or if we have a special exhibition on,' Susan added, by way of clarification.

'And as we needed to speak to Susan anyway, I thought we would see her first before business picks up,' Wild said with a smile. He took a notebook and pen from his jacket pocket. 'Susan, can I introduce Detective Inspector Cassie Rowden from the Cheshire Serious Crime Squad. We are working together on this case.'

'Poor Professor Johan. Who would want to hurt him?' Susan shook her head sadly. 'It's awful. I still can't believe what's happened.'

'You told me on the phone that the professor came in most days for a coffee.' He turned to Cassie. 'If you recall, we have CCTV of the professor and the murdered priest in here.'

'Yes, he came in most days about ten thirty, for a coffee and a cake,' said Susan. 'He had a bit of a sweet tooth, did the professor. His office is on this floor, so he didn't bother going anywhere else when he could get food and drinks here for a fraction of what he would pay in town. Quite a lot of the staff do the same. Saves them time and money.'

'So the last time you saw him, was he alone?'

'No. He came in with a priest, like you said. He ordered for both of them and they sat right in the corner, out of the way.'

'Had you ever seen this priest before?' asked Cassie.

Susan shook her head.' No, I would have remembered.

Professor Johan was usually on his own. Always had his crossword with him, or he was on his laptop.'

'How long were they in here?' asked Wild.

'Not long. They talked for a while, heads together, like they were afraid someone might be listening, and then the priest got up and left. He didn't even drink his tea.'

'How much longer did the professor stay?' Cassie enquired.

'He did finish his coffee, but then he left too. He usually had a good half hour, but I'd be surprised if he was here ten minutes that day. He didn't even say goodbye, just went.'

'And normally he would say goodbye?'

'Why, yes, Chief Inspector. He would put everything on his tray, bring it to the counter, say how much he had enjoyed his cake and then go. Such a lovely man.'

The room was silent as they reflected on this.

'Thanks, Susan,' said Wild, 'that's very helpful. We won't keep you any longer.'

The woman got up and smiled at them both.

Once they were alone, DCI Wild pulled the plate of scones over.' Want one? 'he asked as he took one and cut into it.

'Maybe later. The CCTV footage you sent me, that's all we have of the priest? None anywhere else?'

'Got my crew on it at the moment. We know he left the museum straight after his meeting with the prof, but then he seems to disappear. 'He took a bite of his scone. 'This is lovely,' he said, spitting a few crumbs as he spoke. 'You're missing a treat here, Cassie.'

'Who else are we seeing?' She took out her pad and pen.

Wild licked his fingers. 'Let me see. Dr Lora Findlay, one of the professor's colleagues, who worked closely with him on The Book. Jessica Tong, his secretary, and Truman Gryfinn. He used to work here, and was a close friend of Professor Johan.'

He finished his scone, then licked his fingers again and wiped them on his napkin. 'Sorry about the finger-licking thing. Bad habit of mine – drives my wife mad.' But he had the smile of a man who didn't care what other people thought about him, ever.

CHAPTER FIVE

'I don't know what Johan's lead was,' said Dr Findlay. 'He was so secretive over that book. I mean, he only had a tiny part of it.'

'The part he photographed when he was with me?' asked Cassie.

'Possibly. When he was at the Warrington police station. He wouldn't let me see it at first, not even a peep.' Dr Findlay was tall, thin and very serious-looking, with dark-framed glasses perched on the end of her nose. Her blonde hair was held off her face with a hair claw. She wore a blue suit with a white shirt, and heels so high that Cassie wondered if they gave her a nosebleed when she walked. She didn't seem that perturbed about her colleague's death, and professed to know nothing about why he was going to Malta.

'One of my detectives told me that you collaborated closely on this project with the professor,' Wild said, with none of the warmth he had shown towards Susan.

'That came after the copy of the artefact was stolen. He was so secretive about the whole thing until then. That's when he asked for my help – when he realised he wouldn't get the entire manuscript. All of a sudden it was urgent. I spent hours, weeks trying to decode what he had, but it was beyond me. And beyond him too.' It was as if she had to prove herself as good as the professor.

'Someone was brutally murdered when The Book was stolen,' said Cassie, 'and now the professor is dead. Maybe he was just trying to protect you.'

'Protect his findings, more like.' She rolled her eyes at the detectives' expressions. 'What?' She looked down at her clasped hands.' Everyone in academia is after the next big thing. It brings prestige, book offers, tours, guest lecturing, promotion. If that book had been the real deal, a genuine copy of The Book of

Sceleratis, it would have been almost as good as finding the Holy Grail. I'd certainly kill for it.' As soon as the words were out, she realised what she had said. 'Not actually kill. I wouldn't really kill anyone. It's a saying. I didn't mean kill.' Her face was flushed.

DCI Wild looked down at his notebook, then back to her.' But you think the book is possibly why he was killed?' he asked quietly.

'Well, yes. I mean, people have died, as your colleague DS Rollen pointed out.'

'DI Rowden,' said Cassie.' Dr Findlay, please fill me in on why this find is so important. When I met the professor, he talked about the Knights Templar escaping from the Far East with holy relics.'

'Yes, they did: we know that. What we don't know is where said relics ended up, and why they were never recovered. The Book of Sceleratis was found in a dig in Egypt and copied in code, then disappeared. The original may have been destroyed.' She shrugged.' We will probably never discover whether it still exists. But this copy gave us some information from the original.'

'And what do you expect it to reveal?' asked Wild.

Dr Findlay shrugged again. 'Some say it holds the word of God, like the Ten Commandments, but through his vessel: his son.'

Cassie gasped.' What, it was written by Jesus?'

'Why not? The Dead Sea Scrolls were written by learned men before Christ was born. And even if you don't believe in Christ being the son of God, he was a learned man whose teachings have shaped our lives for thousands of years.' Her eyes glazed over. 'The Book could answer so many questions. If we ever see it again, that is. And the other two people who had seen that tiny fragment of the copy are both dead.'

'You mean Professor Johan and Dr Dolenz, I take it?' asked Wild.

'Yes. I worked with Dolenz: he was a fellow here for several years before he returned to his home country. He wanted to carry on with his research on the Knights.'

'The Knights Templar?' asked Cassie.

'Yes. He was convinced that they are still active – but underground, in secret.'

'And what is your opinion of that theory?' The DCI leaned forward, giving the doctor his full attention.

'I think the closest thing you will see of the knights these days are a few sad men who dress up and call themselves Freemasons.'

Cassie Looked at Dr Findlay. 'You have just stated that the other two people who had looked at pages from the copy are now dead.. Please be careful Doctor.'

'Do you think I might be in danger?' Dr Findlay paled.

'We will look at getting some protection for you,' said Wild. 'Please don't go anywhere without clearing it with us first.' He closed his notebook.

'What, I can't go anywhere?' She sounded both aggrieved and shocked.

'Within reason you can, but just let us know, for your own safety.'

Dr Findlay unwound herself from the seat and with a last glare at them, left.

'What do you make of her?' murmured Cassie.

'Not much,' the DCI replied, slightly louder than necessary. Cassie winced, hoping Dr Findlay hadn't heard. 'Right, I'm off to the little boys' room for a comfort break. Be a love and grab another couple of drinks, will you? We have Miss Jessica Tong next, the professor's admin assistant. Let's see if she's as cold as that one.'

***

Wen was balancing Daisy gently on her knee at the same time as trying to use her laptop. It made her feel slightly nauseous. However, every time the motion stopped the baby complained.

During her conversations with Professor Johan, Wen had been gradually sucked into his world. A world of knights fighting battles in foreign lands, going on quests for good, amassing huge fortunes and hiding holy relics. She needed more information, but a Google search had shown hundreds of sites. Where to begin?

She had just clicked on an interesting article:' The Knights Templar: still with us? Truth or myth?' It talked about the Military Order of Christ which had taken over in Portugal from the Templars in 1318. While the Knights had gone in and out of favour, the order still existed in some form. Many sources said it was just a honorary title, sitting with the military, while others said the order was still active and existed to protect the Holy Catholic Church.

The link with Malta was even more sketchy. The paper said the Knights of Malta should not be confused with the Templars, but Wen was sure Professor Johan had said they were linked, and that the Knights of Malta had helped their brethren escape from Philip IV of France and Pope Clement in 1307.

Johan had said that it really did depend on which academic article or book you read. Different 'experts 'had so many views on the history of the Templars after 1307, and of course they all thought they were right.

Daisy wriggled, then grizzled, and started winding up to a full hearty cry. Wen decided she would return to her research later. Maybe tonight, if her baby daughter decided to sleep for any length of time.

She stood up, holding Daisy close, and rocked her. She couldn't make sense of what was going on. Could these three murders be connected, and if so, how and why? There were so many questions, and answers would be hard to come by.

***

Jessica Tong sat opposite the two detectives. She was beautiful, petite, nervous, and at least partly East Asian.

DCI Wild smiled, trying to put her at her ease. 'Now, Jessica... It's OK to call you Jessica, I take it?' She nodded. 'Good. We just want some background information on the professor, please.'

She nodded again, hiding behind her cloak of dark hair.

'How long did you work for the professor?' asked Cassie.

The girl pulled the cuff of her sleeve and looked up, as if trying to get inspiration from the space above their heads.' Er, about two years, I think.'

'Did you like working for him?' Cassie sensed this interview would be like pulling teeth.

Jessica nodded again.

Wild took over. 'When did you last see him?'

'Er, the day before he left for Malta. Well, I mean, the day before he was due to leave for Malta.' She still hadn't made eye contact, and was obviously finding this difficult.

'And was he himself, do you think?' Wild was tapping his pen on the table, which wouldn't help Jessica relax. And it was starting to aggravate Cassie.

'I think so.'

'Good,' said the DCI, between gritted teeth.

'Though he was a bit sharp with me, and he wasn't like that. Always nice, really nice.' She wiped her eyes on her cuff.

Cassie produced a tissue and offered it to Jessica. 'Thank you,' she murmured, sniffing.

'Any idea why he was snappy that day?' Cassie asked, giving Wild a look which made him stop tapping his pen.

'He couldn't get the flight he wanted. He wanted to go that evening, like straight away, after the phone call.'

'Which phone call?' The DCI had returned to his softly-spoken self now that his interviewee was producing proper sentences.

'From his friend in Malta. He asked me to book him on a flight that evening, and the earliest I could get him was the next morning. He kept saying it might be too late, that time was of the essence and they might already be on the trail.'

'Did he say who might be on what trail?' DCI Wild now looked very interested.

'No. He was sort of babbling: he did that sometimes. Then he put some papers in his bag, took his laptop and left.' Jessica's words were coming in gasps as she fought back her tears.

'Yes, he did do that. Babble, I mean,' said Cassie, remembering how she had tried to keep up with Professor Johan's train of thought during the one and only time she had met him.

'Anything else you can think of?' asked Wild.

Jessica shook her head.

'OK, that is all for now. You have my card if you think of anything else.'

She nodded and got up to go. But at the door, she turned. 'There was one thing.'

'What was that?' asked the DCI as he wrote in his book.

'A priest. Said he knew the professor.'

Both Cassie and Wild looked at her.' A priest?' Cassie said quietly. 'Someone you knew?'

'No, I'd never seen him before. He called after the professor had left that day and said something really odd. Something like, "They know – I've got to warn him about the priory." I said I'd try the professor's phone, but the priest told me he would go to his flat and speak to him. Then he left. But I don't suppose that's got anything to do with what happened.'

CHAPTER SIX

Detective Constable Ruby Wall pushed herself away from her desk, deciding that she needed caffeine, or rather more caffeine. 'I'm getting nowhere with this priest. No one has reported a vicar, priest, curate, or any other man of the cloth missing. I've even contacted different dioceses around England to enquire if anyone has gone AWOL – not returned from a holiday perhaps – and nothing.' She said this to no one in particular, but hoped that Detective Sergeant Colin Briggs, her partner and superior officer, had taken notice.

'Want a coffee, Col?' Ruby asked as she got up.

'No, thanks.' Colin was checking CCTV footage from Merseyside Police, trying to find out where the elusive priest had gone after he left the World Museum, and he was beginning to see double. 'Join the police force, they said. Exciting and glamorous, they said,' he muttered.

Jake, the unit's IT guru, poked his head out from his bank of screens. 'I'll have a coffee, Rubes, if you're offering.'

'Get it yourself, Jake, you're not crippled. Er, not any more.' Ruby flinched inwardly as she realised what she had said.

A pen hit the back of her head as she went to the machine. Jake was a left-side amputee, who now walked, ran and did what everyone else did with the aid of a very posh prothesis. He liked that Ruby didn't tiptoe around the subject, unlike many of his other colleagues.

As Jake got up, he also moaned at the lack of progress. He was searching ports, train stations and airports to see if they could pin down if the priest had come into Liverpool, and if so, when. The all-points bulletin had given them no leads, and now they were waiting for a cleansed photo of the dead man. The ones taken at the scene wouldn't have helped, as his face was so badly beaten.

A uniformed officer knocked on the open door.' Excuse me, Sarge.'

Colin paused the CCTV.' Yes?' he said, relieved to have a break from the computer.

'There's a Lee Nelson downstairs. Says he was asked to come in to give a statement on the body he found at the priory.'

'Oh, right, 'said Colin, getting up and stretching. 'Thank you, I'll be right there. Can you show him into interview room two, please?'

Ruby returned to her desk.' I'll get this for you, Colin,' she said, reaching for her notebook.

'Thank you, Ruby, but I need a break.' Colin indicated to his screen.

'Well, can I come too? 'She looked at Colin intently.' Please?'

'Oh, all right. 'She grabbed her book and a pen and Colin gave her a warning look.' But I'm leading the interview.'

Ruby smiled. 'Of course.'

'No, Ruby, I mean it.' They left together.

'Does Colin put up with Ruby's behaviour because she failed her sergeant's exam and he passed, do you think? 'asked one of the officers to no one in particular.

'No,' said Jake.' He's just nice.'

'Mr Nelson.' Colin held out his hand to a nervous-looking man, who rose and wiped his hand on his trousers before taking it. The hand was still slightly clammy, and Colin had to resist the urge to wipe his own hand. Instead, he introduced himself and Ruby. 'Please sit down, Mr Nelson.' Colin indicated the seat the man had just risen from.

The man sat back down. 'Lee, please. No need for formality. I feel as if I'm at work.' He gave a strained laugh.

Lee Nelson was in his mid-forties, tall and thin with a goatee. His thinning hair was slightly too long and brushed back from his face. He was dressed in a smart suit, shirt and tie. Colin wondered why Lee Nelson needed to stress that his job had enough significance to warrant use of his formal title. 'And what is it you do for work?'

'I work at Daresbury. The research facility. Do you know of it?'

'Yes, I know it,' said Colin. 'It has that odd tower-looking thing.'

'The Daresbury tower. Yes, it is quite a landmark, isn't it?'

'What's it used for?' asked Ruby.

'I could tell you, but then I'd have to kill you,' Lee said, with the same irritating laugh, then looked at his feet. 'Sorry, that's inappropriate in the circumstances.'

'What is it you do there?' asked Colin.

'I'm a research scientist in nuclear physics.'

'Oh. That sounds... 'Colin looked at Ruby.

'Complicated,' she finished.

'Yes, very complicated.' Lee smiled.

'But you enjoy your job?' Colin asked. Lee nodded. 'Right. Now, Lee, can you tell me how you came to find our victim, please.'

'Yes, of course. Well, you see, I live not far from the priory and I always run through the grounds. It was five forty-five am when I left home and about six when I got to the priory. I saw something out of the corner of my eye, but it was slightly misty and I couldn't make out what it was. As I got closer, I thought someone had sacrificed an animal on one of the large flat stones. Apparently, it's happened in the past. Black magic, witchcraft, that sort of thing. But as I got closer... 'Lee swallowed.

'Would you like some water?' Ruby asked, already halfway out of her seat. He nodded and closed his eyes. Ruby went to the water dispenser and fetched him a drink.

'Sorry, Lee, I know this must be very distressing for you,' said Colin. 'I've only seen the photos of the crime scene and that was bad enough. Just take your time.'

He nodded again and took a few sips of water.' I'm fine, thank you. As I said, I went closer and then realised there was a human body on the stone, covered in blood and,' he shut his eyes, 'and nailed to a piece of wood. It was awful.' He took another sip. 'I'm embarrassed to say that I vomited. And then I called the police. It didn't occur to me until much later that I didn't check to see if he was alive. Isn't that terrible? It's been bothering me ever since. He might have still been alive.' He trembled, clearly close to tears.

'I think you should take a break, Lee,' said Ruby. 'I'm going to get some coffee for myself – would you like a warm drink too?' Ruby was being her gentlest self, a side to her which people didn't often see.

'A black coffee would be more than welcome, thank you.'

'OK. How about you, Colin?'

'No thanks, I'm good.' She left, and Colin resolved to pull her up later about addressing him by his first name when they were with members of the general public. It was just about all right in the office, though their colleagues looked skyward when she spoke to him. But it wasn't appropriate when they were interviewing.

'Do you live alone, Lee?' Colin reverted to general questions, hoping that would give Lee time to recover before going back to the gory details.

'No, I live with my wife. She's a teacher at the local primary school. We have a nice house at Windmill Hill.'

'And how long have you lived there?'

'Let me see, it must be coming up to five years. Next month, to be exact. It was when I got the job at Daresbury. We lived in London before that.'

'And where did you work there?'

'I was working for the Ministry of Defence and Lilly – Elizabeth, my wife – was doing her teacher training.'

'You were a spook? 'Colin said, laughing.

Lee said nothing, and an uncomfortable silence fell.

Colin was glad when Ruby returned a few minutes later with a drink for their witness and one for herself. He didn't know why she wasn't stick thin and jittery, given all the caffeine she put away during the working day. 'We'll push on, if that's all right with you, Lee? Get this completed. I'm sure you want to put this behind you and get on with your life.'

Lee looked deep into his coffee cup.' I don't think my life will ever be the same again,' he said quietly.

Ruby and Colin exchanged glances. 'Can I just ask, was anyone about when you went for your run?' Colin said. 'Did you see anything out of place? Unusual?'

He looked up. 'I can't think of anything, except...' His gaze went faraway again, as if he was trying to remember. 'A car.'

'A car? Can you describe it?'

'It was a people carrier. Black, with black windows. The sort you can see out of when you're in the vehicle, but people outside can't see in.'

'And why was it out of place?' said Ruby.

'It was parked up the road from the priory. I don't usually see parked cars there at that time of the morning. Cars going past, yes, but not stopped. And I'm sure I heard it drive away as I got close to the body.'

Colin looked at him. 'Did you tell the officers on the scene about this?'

'No, I didn't. I was so upset that I forgot all about it. I'm sorry. Could it be important?'

'It's just something we need to look at, so that we can exclude whoever it was from our enquiries. They might have seen something important.'

They went over a few more points with Lee, and then the interview was over.

'I'll get these notes onto the computer, print out a copy for you to read and sign, and then you can go. Thank you once again for coming in. You've been very helpful.' Colin stood up. Ruby smiled at Lee and followed her sergeant to the door.

'I had to throw my running shoes away,' Lee Nelson said.' I'd only just broken them in, but they were covered in blood. They had his blood all over them.'

'You're joking. 'Ruby stared at her colleague, trying to work out if he was playing a practical joke on her. 'Him. A spook?'

'He said he'd worked for the Ministry of Defence in London while his wife did teacher training.'

'Well, I hope he's never captured and interrogated for secret information. He wouldn't last two minutes.'

'Not all His Majesty's secret servants work in the field, you know. He probably just did stats for them.'

'Who did what where?' asked Jake, always ready for a gossip.

'We reckon the chap who found the body at the priory was a spook in a past life.'

'Which is hard to equate with the quivering wreck we've just spoken to,' said Ruby, with a grin.

'What's his name? Give me his details and I'll check.' Jake grabbed a scrap of paper and a pencil from Colin's desk, ready to take down information.

'Er, excuse me?' said Colin, with as much authority as he could muster.' Haven't you heard of something called the Data Protection Act?'

'We're the police.' Jake was not about to give up on something more interesting than searching flight manifestos for a man whose name he didn't know, who might or might not be a priest.

'Don't poke the bear, Jake,' said Colin.

'It's me they'll take to the Tower. Come on, Sarge, you know you want to. Background information, might be relevant to the case. We do it all the time.'

Jake was right. They did background checks on people who could be relevant to a case without getting permission, but was it OK for a witness who had just found a dead body? Could he be more involved than he was letting on?

'Oh alright.'

'Yay!' Jake did a little fist-pump, then put on his serious face. 'In that case, give me his name, address and date of birth and I'll have a look and see.'

'OK, but I want you to be discreet. Could be sensitive.'

'Don't worry, I can be discreet,' Jake said, as he headed to his desk with a smile on his face.

CHAPTER SEVEN

'Last one, then we'll head for the professor's home,' DCI Wild said as he wiped his mouth. 'That was very nice,' he declared of the salmon and cream cheese bagel which Susan had brought in as Jessica Tong took her leave.

Cassie consulted her notes. 'So, this is Truman Gryfinn?'

She had struggled to keep up with her colleague, who seemed to rush his interviews. When she pointed out that they hadn't asked Dr Findlay if she had seen this so-called priest, he shook his head. 'Already been asked, when my DS set up the meeting. She said no. Young Jessica was off sick until today – shock, apparently – but I should have brought it up during our interview. That'd be a fail in Detective Training 101.' He laughed, but Cassie suspected he felt these interviews were a waste of time.

'And Truman Gryfinn was a friend and ex-colleague of the deceased?'

'So we've been led to believe.'

As he finished speaking, there was a knock at the door and a man popped his head in. 'Are you ready for me? Your officer said about one.'

'Certainly, sir, come in.' Wild stood up, while Cassie pushed their lunch debris onto the tray and parked it on another table.

Truman Gryfinn was tall, of African-Caribbean background, with short grey hair, and he wore a well-tailored three-piece suit. In his hand he held a fedora. He was a walking fashion statement, which said, 'I might be getting on, but I have style and I'm not afraid to show it.'

Wild indicated a chair on the other side of the table. 'Please take a seat, Mr Gryfinn.'

'It's Professor, actually. Just so you can make your official notes correct.' He smiled as he sat down.

'Professor, sorry. I'm Detective Chief Inspector Wild, Liverpool Murder Team, and this is my colleague, Detective Inspector Rowden from the Cheshire Serious Crime Squad. Thank you for your time. I believe you and Professor Johan were good friends. We wondered if you could fill us in on anything you know that might pertain to his murder.'

Truman looked grim.' Anything I can do, I shall. I still can't believe he's dead, you know. We communicated most days – text, emails, phone calls – and ate together once a week. It's been very hard to accept.'

DCI Wild nodded sympathetically. 'It must have been a terrible shock for you, but we need to push forward with this case while it's fresh in people's minds. When did you last speak to Professor Johan?'

'The day before he died. He was very upset. He said a priest had been to see him, here at the café. The priest warned him against carrying on his search for The Book.'

Both Cassie and Wild sat up. 'Did he say why the priest was warning him off, and who he was?' Cassie asked.

'All he said was that this man appeared at his usual coffee time, sat down at his table, and pleaded with him to drop his quest. He said only terrible things would come from finding and decoding the artefact.'

'And what did the professor say to that?' this came from Cassie.

. 'He informed him that nothing would stand in the way of the truth, whatever that ended up being. Then he told him to go away.'

'Apparently the priest returned later to warn the professor about the priory,' said DCI Wild. 'Any idea what that was about?'

Truman looked confused.' No, but wasn't a man found dead there, the same day as— Good God, was that the priest? I didn't make the connection.' He looked at them, eyes wide, and Cassie saw something in Truman Gryfinn's face that hadn't been there before: naked fear.

***

As they headed towards Sefton Park, Cassie and Wild discussed the last interview.

'So when the priest warned Professor Johan about the priory, do you think he meant Norton Priory?' asked Cassie. 'And if he did, is he the priest who was found there, and why did he go?'

'Well, little Jessica made it sound more like a thing or an organisation than a place,' said Wild. 'But that's just an afterthought, really. The priest could have been talking about the place. The priory is a place of danger, the priory is a meeting place, the priory is… Damned if I know, Cassie. What do you think?'

'I think it's a group or collective of people who don't, for whatever reason, want anyone to see this artefact. I mean, we have three murders here. Four if you include Jeff Morgan, and we should, because he died trying to get The Book to the professor. Person or persons unknown are going to an awful lot of trouble to conceal this item.' Cassie sighed. It was still all conjecture and hearsay.

The DCI's phone rang and he answered using his Bluetooth speaker. 'Talk to me.'

'Sir, IT have managed to unlock the professor's laptop.'

'Good stuff. Anything useful?'

'Well, in an email to Dr Carlo Dolenz, the professor says he's traced the original Book of Sceleratis.'

'I thought that had been destroyed,' said Cassie.

'So did everyone else, by the sound of it,' said the person at the end of the line.

'Thanks.' Wild ended the call. 'That makes things more interesting, I suppose. If this book is still in existence.'

'Real deal or copy, I don't see the difference,' said Cassie. 'Someone is still prepared to kill to keep it out of the public domain.'

Professor Johan's flat was part of a compact building with four turrets, one at each corner. Set in well-manicured gardens and backing onto a park, it was a very pleasant locality.

The police officer on the door tipped his cap to the DCI as they entered. Cassie was surprised at how modern the decor was. Lots of white, and fitted furniture. The pale carpet made the bloodstain look even worse, and she kept well away from the dark-red marks.

There was a bedroom with its own bathroom, a separate toilet and shower room, a kitchen-diner, and a small sitting room in the turret. There, the professor had placed a comfortable chair, small table and reading lamp, and on one wall was a floor-to-ceiling bookcase. Another room was a study, which could have doubled up as a guest bedroom if needed. There were papers on the floor, books on chairs, and a large desk with a clean space where his laptop would usually sit.

'When uniform got here, he was dead in the hall,' said Wild. 'The door was slightly open; his bag was on his bed and nothing had been touched.'

'Who found him?'

'Taxi driver. We think the killer heard him coming and rushed off. Otherwise, surely they would have searched the place, and at the very least taken his laptop.'

Cassie nodded as she examined her surroundings. 'Don't these places have locked front doors and CCTV?'

'They do, but people on their way out often don't wait for the door to lock behind them. And the CCTV was vandalised last week. That in itself is strange.'

'Why?'

'These flats have been here for almost ten years, and this is the first time it's happened. A week before a murder. That makes me twitchy.'

They donned gloves and began to poke around, looking for a clue that even a thorough crime scene team might have missed. It was unlikely, but sometimes fresh eyes see things from a different perspective and come across a clue forensics hadn't noticed, which they would get very shirty about. But today nothing popped up or looked strange to either of them.

As they walked back to the car, Cassie looked at her watch. 'Would you mind dropping me back at the railway station, please? I can make the five to if we don't get held up.'

'We won't,' said Wild.

Every rule in the safe driving handbook went out of the window as they hurtled along, blues and twos going. 'There's really no need, 'protested Cassie, clutching the grab ring over the door.

'I know,' said the DCI, 'but it's fun.'

Cassie thanked DCI Wild and ran up the steps of Lime Street Station. Not because she was cutting it fine, but because she wanted the public to think the sirens and lights had been necessary. Once she was in the station, she blended with the public and got her breath back.

She had a good fifteen minutes before her train was due, so she gave Wen a call and brought her up to speed.

'There might be one or two leads there,' Wen said, thoughtfully.'I'll pop in tomorrow and we can go through your notes more carefully. I was going to join the Zoom meeting from here, but if Aran doesn't mind, I'd rather be in the office.'

'Something was found on the professor's computer that you might be interested in. No, you *will* be interested in. About The Book.'

Wen was all ears.' What?'

'The professor's emails to the doctor in Malta said he had a lead on the original artefact.'

'But didn't the professor say that had been burnt?'

'Yes. But when you think about it, it's all conjecture and conspiracy theory. No one knows for sure.'

'Smoke and mirrors,' Wen said quietly.

CHAPTER EIGHT.

Wen left Daisy with Aran bright and early the next day. Neither she nor her baby had slept well, and Wen got up just after five, realising there was little chance of sleep now.

By the time Aran came down for breakfast, Wen had Daisy dressed and fed. Her bottles had been prepared and put in the fridge. 'And finally, she sleeps,' said Wen, looking at her brother's face. He was bright-eyed and bushy-tailed, as always.

'Isn't it strange,' she said, as she looked down at her daughter sleeping peacefully in the Moses basket. 'Even when you're absolutely knackered because of your baby, as soon as they sleep you just want to stand and watch.'

'You might want to, but I don't. Go on, off to work with you, and don't forget to come home.' Aran almost pushed her out of the front door.

In the DI's office, Wen and Cassie read the extensive notes she had taken the previous day, now typed up in a neat document.

'So, of the people you met yesterday, who do you think might be involved in this case?' asked Wen. 'If anyone, that is.'

'It's easier to say who definitely isn't involved,' said Cassie. 'In my mind, that's Susan and Jessica.'

'I agree. Dr Findlay and Professor Gryfinn could know more than they're letting on. Dr Findlay would achieve career progression and all that goes with it, while Professor Gryfinn would make a monumental discovery in the world of artefacts and religious history. Definitely something to be remembered for.'

'But would they kill for that? And would they kill four people, including one in another country?'

'Probably not. But they might be feeding information to the real criminals.' Wen shook her head.' I need coffee. My lovely daughter was awake most of the night.'

'Coming up. Biscuits?'

'Definitely.'

As Cassie rose from her seat, there was a knock and Jake entered.

'Don't you ever wait for a "come in", Jake?' snapped Cassie.

'What? Sorry, boss. But I've got some important info on one of the witnesses. Well, *I* think so.'

Cassie sat back down. 'And what is it?'

'The man who found the body.'

'Yes, er... 'Cassie paged through her notes, looking for his name.

'Lee Nelson,' Jake said.

'Yes, Lee Nelson. Is there a problem with him?'

'There might be. I've done a history search on him, and as far as I can tell, he doesn't exist!'

Colin sat back; legs crossed. Ruby was at his side with her usual smile, happy, relaxed and natural. Nothing seemed to alter Ruby's demeanor. She was always calm, and reasonable.

'What made you want to do a check on this man?' asked Wen.

'He was very nervous. On edge,' Colin replied.

'Well, he had come across a very gruesome murder. That would upset most people, wouldn't it? We tend to forget what that can do to someone's mental wellbeing because we take it in our stride, most of the time.'

'Yes, boss, but he was edgy. He looked ... he looked...'

'Guilty,' said Ruby.

'Did he?' asked Cassie.

'Yes,' said Colin. 'That's exactly the impression he gave. Not necessarily because he'd committed a murder, but he was definitely hiding something. He also said that he'd seen a black people carrier parked close to the priory, which we're looking into.'

'And there was the other thing, too,' put in Ruby.

'What other thing?' Cassie tried not to frown. Ruby was a good detective, but her love of melodrama could be trying.

'He'd been a spy.'

'What?!' exclaimed Cassie and Wen.

'Now we don't know that, not for sure,' Colin said hastily.

'What *do* we know?' Wen sat up straight and looked at the pair with her best 'I'm the boss' face.

'I asked him how long he'd lived and worked in Runcorn and he said five years. When I asked him what he'd done previously, he said that he'd worked for the Ministry of Defence while his wife trained to be a teacher. I pushed him on that, just in a light-hearted manner, but he didn't say any more.'

Wen and Cassie looked at each other, then back to Colin and Ruby.

'So I asked Jake to do a background check,' Colin continued, 'taking all things into consideration, and it came up blank. Lee Nelson didn't exist until five years ago, when he started working for the nuclear research facility at Daresbury.'

Wen tapped her pen on the table. 'Right. Colin, get in touch with the HR department at his place of work and see if they'll fill in his backstory, though that's unlikely. Ruby, try and find out more about his wife. Be careful, though. We don't want to ring any alarm bells.'

Colin and Ruby left the office.

'Sorry if I jumped in there, Cassie,' said Wen.

'No, not at all. What do you think is going on with Lee Nelson, then?'

'He could actually be a spy – but if so, who for? Or he could be in witness protection. Even so, usually he'd have a false history. Either way, we need to tread carefully.'

The Zoom meeting went ahead as planned. Each party had more information to share, though Warrington and Liverpool were offering the same intelligence. Cassie and Wen had decided beforehand to keep a lid on the development with Lee Nelson, apart from his revelation about the car he'd seen.

'Do you think it might be significant?' asked DCI Wild.

'We thought that while your staff are trawling through CCTV footage, it might be of use,' said Cassie.

'Here in Malta, we have managed to decipher some of the documents on Dr Dolenz's laptop,' said Luca. 'They confirm that he thought they had a lead to the original book. That is why the professor was in such a rush to get to his friend.'

'Because if he knew...' said Wen.

'Then it wouldn't be long before others did too,' finished Luca.

'So are we presuming that this artefact is in Malta?' asked Cassie.

'Possibly. Or perhaps the professor was meeting his friend there before they went on somewhere else. Dr Dolenz never wrote down the location of this treasure, of course. We are still examining his computer and trying to retrieve deleted files.'

'But he wasn't tortured for information and they didn't get his laptop,' Wen said.

'He actually died of heart failure,' Luca informed them.' I don't think his killer got the chance to ask much, but Dr Dolenz did have bruising on his body. And his laptop was very well hidden. He had given it to his neighbour, saying that if anything happened to him, they should give it to the police.'

'He was scared,' added DCI Wild. 'Wasn't he also stabbed?' This was a statement, rather than a question. 'But why, if he had collapsed?"

'Just to make sure he was dead, I suppose. Or to make the link with Professor Johan's death plain, maybe. These people don't like to leave any loose ends, I'm thinking.' Luca held up his hands. 'Who knows?'

'Who knows indeed, my young friend,' said DCI Wild.

Ruby had asked Jake to do a background check on the wife of Lee Nelson. Her name was Elizabeth, and she also had no past before the couple had settled in Runcorn.

'This is more than odd,' she said to Jake, when he brought the news.

Jake nodded. 'If they're being hidden for some reason, they would both have to have a legend.'

'A which?'

'A past that isn't real. A false history.'

'Get you with your spook terminology,' said Ruby, with a smile.

'I read loads of spy thrillers when I was recovering from surgery. I even had a go at writing one. That's how bored I was.'

'Really? How far did you get?'

'I finished it. Sixty-five thousand words, done and dusted.'

'What?!'

'I was recovering for a long time,' Jake said, tapping his prosthetic leg.

'Did you do anything with it?'

'Like what? Burn it? Use it as a doorstop?'

'Send it to an agent, that sort of thing.'

'What's the point? It's probably a load of rubbish, but it kept me from going out of my tiny mind. I never thought I'd get fed up with playing computer games.' Jake smiled at Ruby.

'Can I read it?'

'No!' His eyes widened. 'What, really?'

'I'd love to.'

'Oh, OK then, but don't say I didn't warn you.' With that, he walked back to his desk. Ruby watched his bottom, thinking, not for the first time, how nice it was.

'Bloody hell.' Colin crashed his phone down. 'I'm getting nowhere with Lee Nelson. Daresbury just keep passing me round. When I finally thought I was getting somewhere, it turns out the person I need to speak to is on long-term sick leave. Or so they say.'

'They're just playing for time, by the sound of it,' said Ruby.

'No shit, Sherlock!'

Ruby goggled at him.

'Sorry, Ruby, but this is so frustrating. Have you had better luck with his wife?'

'The school have given me some information. References, past work history. Not much, really.'

'Well, that's something.'

'It isn't. Jake checked it for me. It's all lies.'

'I think we should pay a call on Mr and Mrs Nelson and give them a nice surprise. What do you think, Ruby?'

Her smile answered his question.

CHAPTER NINE

At the Temple Church in London, one of their ministers was missing.

Father Michael had been on leave for the last three days. He should have taken the morning service today, it being Thursday and Holy Communion.

Father Benedict was called on to take his place, and was annoyed. He had a lunch date and then tickets for *The Book of Mormon*, but no one else could help out.

After the service, Father Benedict made for the Priests house to give Michael a piece of his mind. Christian charity had gone right out of the window. At the very least, Michael could reimburse him for his theatre tickets.

However, when he reached his destination, there was no sign of Father Michael. Father Benedict knocked at the door, then announced his intention to enter and went in. The rules of the house asked for rooms to be locked only at night, to enable solitude for prayer and meditation before sleep.

The room was as neat as a pin, and when Benedict asked the other residents if anyone knew where Michael was, none could throw any light on his whereabouts.

The disgruntled priest went back to Michael's room, sat on the bed and contemplated the situation. It was very unlike Michael to do this, he had to admit. When Benedict had been asked to fill in at short notice, he had presumed that Michael was unwell until he was told that he hadn't returned from his holiday. Something seemed wrong. He needed to take this higher.

Father Benedict opened a drawer in the bedside table. Inside was some correspondence. He flicked through it, looking for a clue to where Michael had gone, and why. There was nothing of note, and he put the papers back.

He sighed, and picked up the Bible which sat in pride of place on the table. As he thought, he absentmindedly turned the pages until he came across a folded scrap of paper in the middle of the book.

He opened it. On it, in neat handwriting, were the words: 'Finding Sceleratis could end it all.'

***

At last, the facial reconstruction was complete, and the teams had a photo to show people.

'We'll get this in a press release this afternoon. If that doesn't get us any hits, we'll put it on the local and national news tomorrow,' Cassie told her small team.

'Do we know if these three murders are connected or not?' asked Ruby.

'It's too much of a coincidence for them not to be. The professor was on his way to Malta to meet Carlo Dolenz. They were both trying to find the Book of Sceleratis.'

'The one Dr Morgan was killed for?' asked Jake.

'Or perhaps the original. Something on Dolenz's computer suggests that it hadn't been destroyed and could be hidden somewhere, but we don't know if there's any truth in that. What we do know, now that we have the reconstruction, is that the man on the CCTV is definitely the dead man from the priory.' Cassie tapped the grainy CCTV image. 'We didn't want to release that information until we had something more positive to go on.'

Cassie had limited the team on this case until now, as a high-profile case of attempted murder was coming to court soon. Colin, Jake and Ruby had been on the original manhunt for Jeff Morgan's murderer, who had taken the copy of the Book of Sceleratis. She wanted to keep the team small for other reasons too. Safety, security and her trust in them.

'Right, so Colin and Ruby, surprise visit to Mrs Nelson.'

'We're going to call in at the school,' said Ruby. 'But we'll be discreet. Don't worry about that boss.'

'Jake, I want background checks on the people I interviewed with DCI Wild. He knows. He said they haven't uncovered anything amiss, but they haven't got a Jake on their team.'

At this, Jake smiled. Known for bending the rules, he also got results.

'I'm going to the DCI's house this afternoon to try and get somewhere with all this mythology rubbish. And before you go, no one talks about this to anyone outside this room. The press will be hunting for a story. Your reply to such inquiries is…?'

'No comment,' they replied in unison.

'Good. It's important that for now, we keep things close to our chests. Jeff Morgan died because he had a copy of The Book. Our DCI almost died too, and now three others have lost their lives. Whoever's behind this doesn't care who they hurt. It won't bother them that you're police: they will kill you without a second thought.'

The room went quiet as the detectives took up their tasks.

***

'Wen! How are you?' John Baron beamed at Wen, who was standing in the doorway of his office.

'Can I come in?'

'Of course.' He stood up as she entered, looking uncertain, then went in for a hug. Wen felt as if all the air had been squeezed out of her.

John released her and stood back, looking at her. 'It's so good to see you. Tea? Coffee?'

'I'll have a cup of tea, please. I think the palpitations I've been having this morning might be my body telling me not to have any more strong coffee today.'

John put the kettle on and popped teabags in two mugs. 'How are you? I heard you were back.'

'I'm OK. Nothing more, nothing less. And I'm just doing a few hours here and there to support the team.'

'And is Daisy being good for you?' He poured boiling water

into the mugs. 'Milk?'

'Please. She's doing well, but being good? That's a different story. She doesn't sleep at night, hence the dark circles under my eyes.'

John fished out the teabags and after he added a splash of milk, passed Wen her drink. He returned to his desk and looked closely at his friend. 'I think dark circles is a bit of an exaggeration. You look good, considering—'

'Considering I saw the man I loved have the back of his head shot off while I was being strangled? Considering I was put into an induced coma and had a caesarean section during it?' Wen's tone wasn't bitter or sad, just matter-of-fact.

John put his cup down and looked at his feet. 'Sorry.'

Wen touched his arm. 'John, there's nothing to be sorry about. It happened, it wasn't your fault, and I'm pleased to see you too.' They smiled at each other. 'Though I've also come to ask your opinion about the priest.'

'I've done a report – just waiting for a few results...' He hit some keys and the document appeared on his screen. 'Do you want me to email you a copy?'

'That would be useful, but what I really want is to discuss it over a cuppa, like we always do.' She held up her cup. 'Cheers.'

'Good. Right, where to begin. He died from blood loss, from a large incision in his side. But he had also taken a terrible beating. His ribs were fractured, and one had caused his right lung to collapse. His fingernails had been pulled out, and the soles of his feet beaten. Bastinado, it's called.'

Wen winced. 'But who would do that?'

'I don't know, but it's mentioned in the Bible, so it isn't a new form of torture.' John sipped his tea. 'And his hands were nailed to that plank of wood, and a cross burnt into his chest. It all points to some religious crank, if you ask me. But ... I think those last two were done post-mortem. I thought pre-mortem at first, but when I looked more closely at the hands and the brand on his chest, it was more likely to have been just after death.'

'To make a point, maybe?'

John frowned. 'What sort of point, though?'

'Don't mess with us? We are working on behalf of a higher authority?' 'Wen shook her head. 'Who knows?'

***

Colin allowed Ruby to drive. It would stop her chattering quite so much, but she was also a very good driver. It gave Colin time to read the notes they had so far on the mysterious couple, though that wouldn't take long.

As they turned into the road where the school was located, they looked for a parking spot. The school gates were locked and there were so many double-yellow lines around the school that it brought to mind a high-security prison, not a Cheshire primary school.

Eventually, they opted for a side street a good five minutes from their destination, because Ruby ignored Colin's plea to 'Just shove it anywhere, we're police on official duty.'

'And that won't cut any ice with the judge when a small child runs out from behind our ILLEGALLY PARKED CAR and is killed, will it?' Ruby retorted.

When they reached the gate, they had to ring a bell, declare themselves to a camera and show their ID. 'I bet it's fun at home time if every parent has to prove who they are,' muttered Colin, as the gate clicked.

The headteacher, Mrs Silver, met them at the front door, looking most concerned. 'What can I do for you?' she asked, as she showed them into her office. They sat down and Colin and Ruby politely refused refreshments.

Ruby thought Mrs Silver's name suited her very well. Mid-fifties perhaps, slightly overweight, and dressed in a tartan skirt and black jumper. No make-up or jewellery, except her engagement and wedding ring. She had wild grey hair that would have benefited from a good hairdresser.

'Your security is very, er, high-end,' said Ruby, looking at the camera on the wall.

'Yes, well, we had an incident a few years ago. This was the result, I'm sorry to say.'

'What happened?' Colin asked.

'Does that matter?' Her tone was defensive, belligerent. 'Is it anything to do with why you're here?'

'That's for us to decide, Mrs Silver,' said Colin. 'What was the incident, please?'

She deflated. 'Yes, of course. I do apologise. A man – father to one of the children – caused a scene. He was estranged from the child's mother and called here to, well, kidnap his son, not to put too fine a point on it. I brought the child in here and locked the door while the police were called. However, he forced open the door, attacked me, and took the boy.' Her hands were shaking and she was close to tears.

'That must have been very traumatic,' said Ruby, with sympathy. 'How long ago did this happen?'

'Oh, it must be seven years ago now. Hence the extra security.' She took a deep breath and sat up straighter. 'I can't imagine it has anything to do with your visit today, though.'

'No, of course not. Not if it was that long ago. But we needed to check. I'm sorry if it brought up bad memories,' said Ruby softly.

'We'd like to talk to one of your teachers about a current investigation,' said Colin.

Mrs Silver looked pained. 'Wouldn't it be easier to see them at home? I'd rather not have police officers walking the corridors. It reflects badly on the school.'

'We need to see her now, Mrs Silver,' said Ruby. 'Sorry, but it can't wait.'

'Oh, very well.' The headteacher picked up her office phone. 'Who is it you *have* to see so urgently?'

'Elizabeth Nelson,' Colin said.

Mrs Silver put down the receiver. 'In that case, I can't help you. Mrs Nelson has been absent for the last few days. We've had to call in a supply teacher for cover.'

'Is she ill?' Colin asked.

Mrs Silver shrugged. 'We don't know. She hasn't phoned in

sick and no one's answering her landline. And what's more concerning is that her mobile is dead.'

As the detectives drove to the Nelsons' house, Ruby said 'Are you thinking what I'm thinking?'

'That they've done a runner?' said Colin.

'Exactly.'

They pulled up on a drive empty of cars, and the house was silent.

Colin rang the bell, then knocked with some force. He bent down and looked through the letter box. No coats or shoes in the hall: nothing.

'I'll go round the back,' said Ruby.

Colin peered through the window for a better view.

'What do you think you're doing?' said a voice behind him.

Colin turned to see an elderly gentleman gripping a broom. 'And who might you be, sir?'

The man's hold on the broom tightened.' I asked you what you're doing.'

'I'm Detective Constable Ruby Wall and this is my colleague, Detective Sergeant Colin Briggs,' said Ruby, standing at Colin's shoulder with her ID held out. Colin reached for his ID and also presented it to the defender of the property.

The old man relaxed and took a step forward.' Can I see that properly, please?' He took Colin's ID, examined it closely, hummed and hawed, then returned the wallet to its owner, satisfied at last.

'Have you seen Mr and Mrs Nelson today, sir?' asked Colin.

'They left yesterday. Packed both cars to the gunnels and drove off. Lee said it was a family emergency and asked me to keep an eye on the place until they got home.'

'Strange that they packed up both cars, if it was an emergency,' Colin mused.

'I said that, but Lee said it would make things easier when they got there, as he didn't know how long they would be away.'

'Did he say where "there" was? 'asked Colin.

'Dorset: his wife is from that neck of the woods. I have his mobile number – in case of emergencies you understand. I'll just go and get my phone and you can have it.'

Colin waited until the man had walked away. 'Ruby, can you get in touch with the boss and ask her to sort out a search warrant for this place, please?'

'On it.' Ruby moved away from the house, found the right number, and watched the man return, holding up a phone. After taking the number, Colin called Lee Nelson.

'Anything?' asked Ruby.

Colin lowered the phone and shook his head. 'Number discontinued.'

CHAPTER TEN

Wen went home once she had conferred with Cassie, with an agreement that the DI would visit her later, to look at what they had so far and try to think outside the box. She wouldn't have to spend any more time away from Daisy, and she could bounce ideas off her colleague.

But the mass of confusing information was giving Wen a headache, and trying to see patterns in the events was making her more and more frustrated. Working from home was about all she could manage for now. However, going back into the office, and particularly speaking to John, had made Wen realise that there was only so much you could do on your own without going slightly loopy. She had put the same set of data onto her computer twice yesterday, after five hours staring at the monitor, bleary-eyed from lack of sleep.

'Go home, Wen,' John had said, with a smile. 'Hug that baby of yours. Have some lunch, then discuss all this with Cassie later.'

Wen realised that she had often sneaked away to John's office in the past when she was bogged down with a case. It was quiet down there, and no one had caught on to where she was hiding.

John had been one of the first people she warmed to when she started work in the squad. He was straightforward and honest, and for the longest time she had presumed that he was gay. Otherwise, why would such a lovely person not have a woman in his life? He lived alone, that much Wen knew.

He had laughed about that when he found out. They were working on a hate crime, and Wen asked if it had affected him, given his sexual orientation. 'I'm not gay!' he said, when he finally stopped laughing. 'And I wouldn't hide it if I was. I just haven't found the right person yet. And anyway, I'm more than happy with life as it is for now.'

Wen had feasted on beans on toast and milky coffee, prepared by her brother while she fed Daisy and had put her down for a nap, and was sorting out her notes at the kitchen table when she heard the scrunch of a car on the gravel chippings of the drive. She put the kettle on, then went to open the door.

'They've bloody gone,' said Cassie, as she entered the hall.

'Who's gone?' Wen asked, taking Cassie's coat.

'The bloody Nelsons. Colin and Ruby went to the wife's place of work.'

'The school?'

'The school. No sign of her for the last few days, so they went to their home and the pair of them have gone. A neighbour said they packed up both cars yesterday and headed to a family emergency in Dorset. Family emergency my arse.' Finally, Cassie paused for breath.

'Tea or coffee?' Wen asked as the kettle clicked off.

'Coffee, please. Though if I wasn't on duty and driving, I'd ask for a large glass of wine.' Cassie sat down at the kitchen table. 'We've requested for a search warrant for their home and put out an APB with the make and reg of their cars. And now we wait.'

Wen gave Cassie a mug of instant coffee and made herself some Earl Grey, then took a seat next to her colleague. 'They're acting very suspiciously, certainly. But do you think they're involved with the priest's murder, or just running from us?'

'I think they're hiding from someone, and Lee's involvement in this case was just what they didn't need.'

'So why did he report it, and not let someone else find the body?' *This is what I needed,* thought Wen. *This is what I've been missing: working through a problem with someone.*

'Knee-jerk reaction,' said Cassie. 'He was afraid someone might see him and wonder how he didn't see the body.' She put her cup down.' Or he was afraid that whoever killed that man was warning him, and he needed to see if there was a more logical explanation before they went on the run.' Cassie picked up her cup again, with a sigh.' It's all mad, isn't it. None of it makes any sense.' She turned to Wen. 'Any ideas?'

'Drink your coffee. I have some very nice biscuits to go with it.' Wen pushed a cookie jar towards Cassie, whose face brightened. 'And then I'll tell you what I think.'

***

Back at base, Colin and Ruby were writing their reports and waiting for the all-clear to search the Nelsons' house. They had left a local uniformed officer at the location so that no one could tamper with any evidence. There had been no sightings of either car. It seemed as if the pair had vanished into thin air.

Of course, every man and his dog had a theory about the Nelsons' disappearance. These included the Nelsons being Russian spies, or the ringleaders of a sect of black-magic worshippers who had indeed killed the priest.

Colin was on the phone, talking to a police officer in Liverpool about a possible sighting of the priest getting into a black SUV. It was a link to what Lee Nelson had said, though Colin wondered if his claims were questionable now.

Ruby's phone rang. She answered it, listened, then began flapping her free hand at Colin. 'Colin!' she said, through clenched teeth.

Colin turned to her. 'What?' he mouthed.

'Colin, the priest – we know who he is!'

'Sorry mate, I'll have to go. Something's come up. I'll get back to you.' He put down his phone and looked at Ruby, who was still holding her phone with her hand over the receiver.

'He wants to speak to the person in charge, and that's you at the moment.' She held out the phone.

Colin got up, took the phone, and introduced himself. 'Can I help you?'

'I hope so,' said the silky voice on the other end of the line. 'My name is Leonard Deed and I am the Grand Master at the Temple Church in London. One of our priests is missing, and I believe he is the man who has been reported on the news as a murder victim.'

***

Wen and Cassie were on their third drink and the kitchen table was covered in paper. Three laptops were also open, giving off heat and a gentle low hum.

'You think it's all down to this artefact,' said Cassie, as she stretched and yawned.

'I can't see it being anything else. Everything leads back to that book. Jeff's murder, then the murders of the professor and that doctor in Malta.' Wen was typing as she spoke. 'We can't be sure about the so-called priest, of course, but it's a biblical artefact, and that points to his death being connected.'

'What about Rev—'

'What about him?' asked Wen, intent on her screen.

'Have you thought about interviewing him? Or letting me do it?'

'He was interviewed when Jeff was murdered, wasn't he?'

'Yes, but about the attack and the theft of the book. Not about his take on the artefact. Why people are prepared to kill for this book, what it means, how much it's worth. Who would buy it? After all, it was his field before he became a god-botherer.' Cassie reached for her drink and pulled a face as she sipped the cold coffee. 'Can I brew up again, please?' she asked.

'Yes, just help yourself.' Wen sat back and considered what Cassie had just said. 'But wasn't Reverend Fellows asked all this at the time?'

'He was, but all he said was that he had come across the book when he was doing a house clearance and knew it might be worth a considerable amount to the right collector. He also said it could possibly be a fake.'

'That's not the impression I got when we interviewed him about it originally,' said Wen. 'He was scared it might get into the wrong hands. Anyway, if he was looking at it as an item which could make him rich, how come he still had it?'

'That's why I think a prison visit might be a good idea.' Cassie filled her cup and sat back down.

'Would you be happy to question him?' Wen asked. 'He almost killed you. If it hadn't been for John…'

'But he didn't, and believe me, I won't let him get anywhere near me this time. He's still got five years to serve; he should be out in two with good behaviour.' She leaned towards Wen.' We could go together.'

Wen looked at Cassie.' I'll think about it,' she said, as Cassie's phone rang.

'Hello there, Colin. What's occurring?' Cassie sat bolt upright. 'He's sure? In that case, you and Ruby need to get yourselves off to the big smoke.' She hung up. 'We have an ID on our priest, and guess what?'

'What?'

'He was a priest at the Temple Church in London.'

***

Leonard Deed sat back in his chair, cradling a twenty-year-old scotch in a cut-glass crystal tumbler. He contemplated the colour and the smell before sipping the golden liquid. He closed his eyes as he rolled the smoky fluid around his mouth, then felt the fire as it hit the back of his throat.

Sitting by the large window, looking at the garden of the Grand Master's House. The property was far too big for one person and quite beautiful, befitting its title. He had lived here for fifteen years, and they had been the best and worst fifteen years of his sixty-two.

He had met royalty, some of whom he could talk about. He had received ministers of high authority under this roof: even a representative of the Pope recently, seeking reassurance. A reassurance he couldn't give though, because things were spiralling out of control. People were dying because of what he knew, including one of his own priests.

Why had he taken Michael into his confidence? If he hadn't, Father Michael would still be alive. He had cast him adrift on a dangerous sea, and this was the result…

And now he was about to get a visit from the Cheshire Serious Crime Squad.

A knock at his door brought him back to his everyday work, because whatever happened, he still had a job to do. 'Yes?'

The door opened and Leonard's secretary came in. 'Sorry to disturb you, Grand Master,' he said. 'The Dan Brown tour will begin in ten minutes. I believe you are taking the group round today.'

Leonard Deed drained his glass.' I am indeed Mark. 'He stood up, smiled and walked to the door.' Let battle commence.'

CHAPTER ELEVEN

The following day saw the team heading in different directions. Colin and Ruby were taking the six-thirty train to Euston from Warrington Bank Quay, while Wen and Cassie were going to Cumbria. Specifically, to Haverigg prison to see Reverend Fellows, who had been sentenced to six years for actual bodily harm inflicted on a police officer, namely Cassie.

Wen had been furious that the charge wasn't attempted murder. However, the defence had put forward to the CPS that the reverend had been suffering from a mental breakdown at the time of the attack, due to his son's murder, and the CPS had opted for the lesser charge. The reverend had then pleaded guilty, saving the time and expense of a trial.

Cassie, though, hadn't minded. She had been through enough trauma without enduring a trial and everything that went with it.

The two women were delighted that their request to visit Reverend Fellows had been granted at such short notice, but the prison authorities were aware of the seriousness of the crimes under investigation.

They drove into the car park at eleven o'clock on a bright summer's day. Both women got out and stretched: they had been driving for hours, having stopped once for a comfort break and much needed caffeine. At that point, they had swapped seats.

Wen hadn't been sure about leaving Daisy for a whole day. Aran had said that just this once he could manage, but that she wasn't to make a habit of it. 'I knew this would happen,' he complained, when she broke the news the evening before, over supper. 'You just get sucked in Wen. I know work is important to you, but you are a mother now.'

'Am I?' said Wen, wide-eyed. 'Gosh, I hadn't noticed.'

Aran tutted and gave her grudging permission.

'It's made me realise that I need to sort out long-term childcare, and the sooner the better,' Wen had said to Cassie, a few minutes into the journey.

'Not easy, I suppose, leaving your child with a complete stranger,' Cassie said, as she wiped traces of the chocolate she had eaten for breakfast off her hands.

Wen shook her head.' It isn't what we'd planned, Jeff and I. But all I know for sure is that I need my work. I've felt much more like me since I began doing a few hours again. It's what I am, Cassie: a police officer.' She gave her colleague a sidelong glance. 'You've got chocolate round your mouth. I hope you're not going to throw up when we're on the winding roads later.'

'I'll be driving by then, so no problem.'

Now they eyed the high fence surrounding the prison, which was built on an old RAF airfield just outside the Lake District National Park. The category D open prison had come with the Reverend's guilty plea, and offered training, employment, and education.

Once the two detectives were inside, having had their credentials checked and surrendered bags, phones, and any sharp items, they were shown into an interview room. Soon, they heard a key in the door, and Fellows appeared in prison clothes, with a guard. He was a shadow of his former self: thinner, with heavy dark circles under his eyes and thinning, greasy hair.

He smiled at them.' Hello, ladies. How nice of you to come and visit me.' He sat across the table from them. The guard took a seat near the door, already looking bored.

'Hello, Reverend Fellows. How are you?' Wen asked, with no expression in her voice or on her face.

He spread his hands on the table and leaned towards them. 'Just plain old Mr Fellows these days, Detective Inspector Price. The church doesn't approve of their clergy being in prison.'

'It's Detective Chief Inspector now, actually, Mr Fellows,' said Wen.

'Impressive. It would seem that as I have gone down in the

world, you have gone up.' He looked at Cassie.' And you? No longer a sergeant?'

'Detective Inspector these days,' Cassie said, fighting back her dislike for the man.

'Women are taking over the world. Did you know that the governor here is a woman? In a male prison – I ask you. Mind you, she gave me a job in the library and I'm writing a book, so I suppose I shouldn't complain too much.'

He smiled again, and Cassie squirmed involuntarily. 'I must say that I was intrigued by your urgent request to visit me. Must be something important. Normally it's three days 'notice at the very least. However, not many people come to see me.' He paused, as if contemplating his words.' In fact, no one visits me.'

'Don't expect any sympathy from us, Mr Fellows,' said Wen. 'You could easily have been tried for attempted murder.'

'I never wanted to hurt you, Cassie,' he said, looking at his victim.' It was a moment of madness brought on by stress and grief. I'm truly sorry for what happened.'

Cassie didn't meet his eyes, and said nothing in return.

Wen sat back in her chair and tapped the desk with her pen. 'Let's get down to business, shall we, and leave restorative justice for another day.'

'Yes, DCI Price. So, what do you want of me?'

'The Book of Sceleratis?'

As soon as the words were spoken, Fellows sat up, energised. 'Has it been found?'

'You know how it disappeared, then?' Wen asked.

'Of course. I heard that your partner was brutally murdered, and you were left for dead, I believe. The papers just said that a valuable artefact had been stolen, but I had no doubt of what was missing. Then, of course, I was asked about the whole thing by your colleagues. But alas, I wasn't of any help.'

Wen scribbled some notes, more to take her eyes from the reverend and keep herself focused than as a memory aid. Hearing Fellows talk about the incident brought out the worst in her. 'Have you any idea who might have stolen the book?'

'Well, where to begin?' He looked at Wen and laced his fingers together.

'Anywhere would be good,' Wen replied. 'We have nothing at the moment.'

Fellows nodded slowly.' And what would my information be worth to you?'

Wen studied him. 'What do you want?'

'Early release.'

Wen laughed.' Don't push it. As far as I'm concerned, your punishment for that attack was far lighter than it should have been.'

Fellows got to his feet.' I don't think we have anything further to discuss, DCI Price. I'll take my leave of you and wish you a safe journey home.' He made for the door.

Wen held up a hand. 'Just a moment, Bartholomew. Wouldn't you like to be seen by the church as a repentant soul?'

He stopped, and turned.' Believe me, Detective Chief Inspector, the church don't want me talking to you about the sacred Book. In that conversation, hell lies.'

One hour. That was how long their visit had lasted, and forty of those minutes had been spent with the prison governor and the chaplain.

Sarah Montgomery-Smyth, a small middle-aged woman dressed so sharply in tailored jacket and trousers that it wouldn't have surprised Cassie if she had cut herself on her outfit, sat behind an oversized desk which made her appear childlike. She looked at them over the glasses which continually slid down her nose. 'So you didn't get any useful information from Mr Fellows?'

'No, none,' Wen replied. She turned to the prison chaplain, a young man with dark hair, glasses, and a very serious expression. 'Does Bartholomew worship at the prison chapel?'

'He does, every day. He sits and prays, but strangely enough, he doesn't attend the Sunday service.'

'Does he talk to you?' asked Cassie.

'About what?'

'About anything.'

The chaplain shook his head. 'He is polite, but he has never had a conversation with me.' Wen couldn't help thinking that if he smiled, he would be very good-looking.

She turned to the governor. 'He told us that he has never had any visitors. Is that true?'

'I checked when I arranged your visitor passes,' she replied. 'He had a couple of visitors when he first came to us. First a Mr Jones, and four weeks later a Mr Smith came to see him. No one since, until today.' She pushed a printout across the desk. 'Dates and times for your records.'

'Thank you,' said Wen. 'Can you please notify us if he has any more visitors, and also if he does decide that he wants to talk to us.' With that, the two women stood up and took their leave.

'All that way, and what did we get? Not a bloody thing,' said Cassie, as she started the car.

'I wouldn't say that,' Wen replied. 'We know he lied to us about visitors. And come on, Jones and Smith? Who are they trying to kid?'

'I know, but who are "they"?' asked Cassie.

'The church, I suspect. Maybe they just came to tell him he was being defrocked. And maybe they *were* called Mr Jones and Mr Smith, but I'm thinking they came to warn him to say nothing about The Book.'

'You're talking conspiracy theory here. It all sounds a bit cloak and dagger.'

'I've been thinking along those lines since the attack,' said Wen. 'I put it down to shock at first, then post-natal hormones, but then there was that last thing he said before he walked out today.'

'What, about the church not wanting him to talk to us about The Book?'

'Exactly.'

CHAPTER TWELVE

Colin and Ruby stood on the concourse of Euston Station. Colin had been to London only once before, on his brother's stag night. He didn't remember much about that weekend to be honest, apart from being sick in the back of a taxi, then being thrown out of it with his brother by the furious driver.

Ruby, on the other hand, had a sister who lived in London, and was a frequent visitor. Because of this, she had taken command of their journey.

'We need to get onto the Northern Line. That takes us to Embankment, and we can walk from there,' she told Colin. 'But first you need tickets from that machine, or you can use your debit card on the card readers. I've got an Oyster card, but I'm here all the time so it makes sense.'

As they approached the escalators, Colin felt slightly sick. This snake of metal which was taking them into its lair was never-ending. He could feel his pulse quickening. The escalator seemed to go on for ever, taking him into the bowels of the earth. His mouth was dry, and he took some deep breaths to try and calm his anxiety.

As they waited on the platform, Colin loosened his tie. He tried not to panic and make a run for the surface. And when their train pulled in, he felt even worse at the sight of the crowded carriages. But like an unstoppable force, Ruby and the people behind pushed him into the train, and he found himself face to face with a tall man sporting perfect eyeliner and rather fetching pink lip gloss. Colin smiled politely, which got him a smile and a suggestive wink.

'Ruby!' he almost squeaked.

'I'm here, Colin.' She was just behind him. At the sound of her voice he took a deep breath and sighed it out.

Fifteen minutes later, they emerged into the sunshine at

Embankment tube station and Colin gulped fresh air gratefully.

'You didn't like that then,' said Ruby. 'Are you a little bit claustrophobic, maybe?'

'No! I just don't like the whole thing. Noise, dirt, darkness and people. Lots of people. And it's so hot.'

'You get used to it.'

'I wouldn't,' Colin declared, as they set off for the Temple Church. 'Which way?'

'We're in the City of London, between Fleet Street and the Thames. It's a fifteen to twenty-minute walk from here,' replied Ruby, striding ahead.

If it hadn't been for Ruby's eagle eyes, they would have missed the sign that pointed down a small street between two grand buildings facing the Thames.

They passed under various archways, and finally found the church. Colin looked at his watch. 'We're early. Our meeting isn't till ten.'

'Let's go for coffee,' said Ruby.

It didn't take them long to locate a small café nearby. Ruby ordered coffee and cakes for them both, and almost choked when she paid for them.

'I'll bring them over,' said the waitress, with a smile.

Ruby sat down opposite Colin, who was looking at his notebook. 'That was almost twenty pounds!'

Colin looked up. 'What was?'

'Two coffees and two pieces of lemon drizzle cake.'

Colin shrugged.' Well, Rubes, you should know what it costs here. You're the one who's always popping down to London. Anyhow, have you looked around you?'

'I'll give you it's busy for this early.' Ruby glanced around her. 'Oh,' she said, as she saw the black legal robes worn by many of the customers.

'Oh, indeed. We're within spitting distance of the Royal Courts of Justice. I expect this place is a gold mine, and even by London prices they can charge more here and still be busy.'

Colin returned to his notes and Ruby checked emails on her

phone. After ten minutes, the smiley waitress appeared with their coffee and cake. 'Sorry for your wait, we're so busy this morning.'

'No doubt you went to Brazil to pick our coffee beans,' muttered Ruby. The waitress gave her a withering look. Colin glared at Ruby and thanked the waitress profusely.

'We have a list of questions from the boss,' said Colin, as he tucked into the cake.' This is very good,' he said, as he picked up his coffee.

'Which boss?' said Ruby, smiling. 'I'm not sure who we're meant to call boss at the moment. I wonder how they're getting on with Reverend Fellows. The DI said she'd text me when they'd finished.' She put her phone down and sipped her coffee, then made a start on her slice of cake.

The pair sat in companionable silence for the next five minutes, until Ruby could bear it no longer. 'I'm excited about meeting this Grand Master. It should be interesting, if nothing else. Did you know that the title goes back to the Knights Templar in the eleven hundreds?'

'Someone's been doing their research.' Colin smiled and popped the last piece of his cake into his mouth. 'But I did some myself, after the computer games that killer used, that was all Knights Templar and war games.'

'Oh yes,' said Ruby. 'What did you glean from that?'

'The history of the Knights. It was really interesting, actually. It said how rich the Knights were, and how powerful. That's why they were nearly all killed, because they got too powerful. It happened on a Friday the thirteenth. That's why some people consider Friday the thirteenth unlucky.' Colin smiled. It wasn't often he got one over on Ruby.

'Well, it was for them,' said Ruby, and sipped her coffee.

They returned to the church as the clock struck ten. The door was open, and they entered to find themselves fourth in a queue of tourists. They waited patiently as people found cards to pay, tried to locate debit cards on their phones, and asked about becoming friends of the church or whether any discounts were available.

Finally, it was their turn. Colin smiled at the middle-aged lady at the desk. She had light, beautifully styled shoulder-length hair and glasses. 'Can I help?' she asked, in a quiet voice.

Colin showed her his police ID. 'I hope so. I'm Detective Sergeant Briggs and this is my colleague Detective Constable Wall. We have an appointment to see a… 'Colin referred to his notes.' Leonard Deed, please.'

The woman frowned at him. 'That would be the *Reverend* Deed, our Grand Master.'

'And that would be me,' said a voice as smooth as dark chocolate behind them. A man with grey hair and a gentle face, wearing jeans and a cream sweater over a blue shirt, extended his hand.' Welcome to the Temple Church.'

The Reverend Deed led them out of the church and round the corner to a Georgian townhouse. 'This is my official residence, the Grand Master's House.'

Once inside, the Grand Master took them into a large but welcoming sitting room. It had three sofas, all well-worn, but they looked right. There was a large fireplace and heavy curtains at the windows. Curtain ties strained to keep the drapes at bay. He invited them to sit down. 'Tea, coffee?'

'We've just had refreshments, thank you,' said Colin.

'Could I have some water, please?' said Ruby, in a quiet voice. Colin glanced at her; eyebrows raised.

'Of course.' The Grand Master pressed a bell and before he had time to sit down, a man appeared in the doorway.

'Yes, sir?'

'Coffee for one, please. And could we have some tap water and three glasses too, Mark?'

'Certainly sir.' Then he was gone.

'Gosh, is he your butler?' Ruby blurted out, then blushed. 'Sorry. I often say what I should only think.'

The Grand Master laughed.' How refreshing. Does that help or hinder your job? No is the answer to your question. Mark is actually my private secretary, but he will turn his hand to anything. I think he'd even kill for me.' He had a twinkle in his eyes when he said those words.

Ruby glanced at Colin, not sure what to make of that. Colin smiled. 'I'm sorry if I was disrespectful when I asked for you, sir.'

'Not a bit of it. Please, do call me Leo, as we are in private. My full title is Reverend and Valiant Master of the Temple. Our conversation would be never-ending if we went to those lengths.' He laughed.

'Thank you, Leo. And thank you for seeing us. Hopefully we won't take up too much of your time.'

Mark came in, bearing a huge silver tray with their drinks, which he put on a low table in front of Leo. 'Anything else sir?'

'No, thank you, Mark. Just close the door on your way out, please.' The Grand Master reached for his beverage. 'Don't worry about time. Today is my office day, and you are saving my soul from being torn apart by the mundane.' He smiled and sipped his drink.

'Oh, um, good,' said Colin. 'So. Firstly, may we offer our condolences on the death of your priest.'

'Yes. Such a shock, and so horrible. The Deputy Reader of the Temple will travel to Warrington tomorrow to formally identify the poor soul. As far as I know, he was alone in the world. Apart from his holy family, that is.'

'Can you tell us a little about him?' Colin asked. 'His name was Father Michael, I believe.'

'He hadn't been with us that long: about eighteen months. He was still in the Priests' house, but he would have moved into other accommodation before long.'

'Don't the clergy live there as long as they work here?' asked Ruby.

'No. We have a nice place around the corner for our ecclesiastical staff, but it can only accommodate four people. We also put people up there if we have visitors from other churches, presuming we have the room. At the moment we have – sorry, had – two priests living there with a visiting member of the clergy, but he is leaving us soon. For permanent staff, it is usually a stopgap until we can relocate them to other accommodation. How long they stay there depends on what is available. But with the Covid pandemic … well, we all rather stayed where we were.'

'Right,' said Colin. 'Where was he before he came here?'

'Rome: he had spent two years there, studying. But originally, he came from the Republic of Ireland.'

'What was he studying in Rome?'

'The history of Christianity during the Crusades. It was one of the reasons why he wanted to come here. All the history, and particularly the fact that the church was built by the Knights Templar. The history of this building and the knights is fascinating, don't you think?' He finished his coffee and replaced the cup on the tray.

'Would you have called him an expert on the Knights Templar?' Colin asked.

Leo smiled. 'In my humble opinion, an expert is someone who ceases to think because they feel they already know it all. Father Michael was very knowledgeable about his subject. In fact, he had started writing a book about the church and the Knights. Another of many, but they do seem to sell.'

'Do you have any idea why Father Michael was in Liverpool, and why he was murdered in such a way?' Colin leaned back in his very comfortable seat.

'No idea at all, I'm afraid,' said Leo. 'He told his colleagues that he was going to look up some friends from his university days. And as for his death, I have seen this sort of thing before. Satanic rituals. Awful.'

Ruby sat up.' Do you believe in Satan?'

'Of course, Detective Constable Wall. He is all around us, every day.'

'That's about all, I think, Leo,' said Colin. 'Just one more thing.' He spoke slowly, watching the Grand Master. 'Have you ever heard of an artefact called The Book of Sceleratis?' Emotion, he couldn't tell what, passed briefly over the Grand Master's face. 'It was written, so we have been told, by the first Grand Master of the Knights Templar.'

The Grand Master swallowed. 'Yes, I have. Why do you ask?'

'Could you tell us what it is, exactly?'

'It is a holy relic that has been lost for centuries,' the Grand Master said solemnly. 'It is believed by some to be the last written words, not of a Grand Master, but of Jesus Christ himself!'

CHAPTER THIRTEEN

'I'm sorry, but you'll just have to take her with you.' Aran folded his arms across his chest, which meant he was playing hardball. 'I don't mind having her for a few hours now and again. That was the arrangement, Wen. But you're taking advantage of my good nature.'

'You are the only person I trust, Aran. You're so good with her.' Wen tried to think of something that would persuade her brother. 'She behaves much better for you than she does for me.'

Aran said nothing.

'You said the other day that you didn't want her to go to work with me in case she caught something.'

'Now that's just blackmail. But I have things to do, so either you attend the meeting remotely or you take her along.' With that, he went upstairs.

Wen looked down at Daisy, who gazed up at her. 'Oh well, time for you to be introduced to my team Daisy. Today's Bring Your Daughter To Work day.'

Wen had asked Cassie to delay the morning team meeting until nine. That was fine, but Cassie hadn't expected Wen to burst in at nine fifteen, breathless, full of apologies, and lugging a baby in a car seat. Indeed, it was a revelation for the whole team, since their DCI had in the past rebuked staff who turned up late because of childcare issues.

'So sorry, everyone,' said Wen, taking her coat off as she spoke. 'I won't stay long, but I wanted to be here for this briefing and I had no one to look after the baby.' Wen glanced at Daisy, who was already becoming unsettled.

'I'll take her for a while, if you like,' said DC Pinkman, Daisy's namesake.

'Thank you,' said Wen, and handed over her daughter.

She wasn't close friends with Daisy Pinkman, and many were

at a loss as why Wen had called her child after the detective. In fact, the reason was simply that Daisy had been at Wen's bedside when she regained consciousness after the birth.

The police had put Wen under close guard, with a firearms officer outside her room and one of the team with Wen. It just so happened to be Daisy that day.

When the doctor came in to talk to Wen, she asked her if she had chosen a name for her premature baby daughter. 'She's fighting off an infection and she's quite poorly.'

Wen didn't have the strength or heart to think beyond breathing. She looked at her bedside companion. 'Sorry. I know I should know, but I can't remember your name.'

'Daisy Pinkman, boss.'

'That'll do, 'croaked Wen.' Daisy.'

She knew she could change the baby's name later, but Daisy she remained from then on.

Cassie took the lead on the team briefing. The team she had working on the case with was still small, but a few others in the room were paying attention too, this being much more interesting than what they were currently working on.

'Yesterday, the DCI and I took ourselves on a jolly to Cumbria to visit Bartholomew Fellows. We hoped he could tell us who might be behind these events. He was of course questioned after the murder of Dr Jeffrey Morgan and the attempted murder of our DCI here, but at that time he provided no useful information.'

Jake put his hand up.' Why did you think you'd have more luck this time?'

'Fellows has now been incarcerated for several months,' said Wen. 'He has had time to reflect and come to terms with his son's murder and his own actions. It was worth a try. However, he didn't give us anything useful, apart from a parting shot that the church wouldn't want him talking to us.'

'What did that mean?' asked Colin.

Cassie shrugged.' Who knows? What we do know is that he

had two visitors not long after he started his sentence. A Mr Jones, and then separately, a Mr Smith. Yes, I know,' she said to the derisory remarks from the group. 'Jake, can you liaise with Haverigg Prison and see if you can find out more about these mystery visitors. And by the way, Fellows told us he'd had no visitors at all. You have my permission to kick a couple of stones and see what crawls out from underneath. Colin and Ruby, how did you get on?'

Colin stood up and went to the murder board, where he had added some bullet points. 'Ruby and I spoke to the Grand Master of the Temple Church, Reverend Leonard Deed, who was a somewhat formidable presence. He gave us some background on our murdered priest, which is in my report, but he didn't know what he was up to or why he was in Liverpool. Apparently, Father Michael had told colleagues that he was just catching up with some uni friends.'

'Had he heard of The Book? 'asked Wen.

'Oh yes, very much so. He said the legend is that the book contains the last words of Jesus Christ. Maybe the only words Jesus ever wrote.'

Wen and Cassie exchanged glances.

'He also said that if there had ever been such an artefact, the chances were that it had been lost in the mists of time.'

'He actually used those words,' said Ruby.' Such a beautiful voice. I could have listened to him all day.'

'Did he have any idea why someone would kill for it?' asked Wen, feeling as if they were walking in treacle.

'No,' said Colin. 'He doesn't believe the murder has anything to do with that book. He did say that it could have been over another long-lost artefact. Apparently, these things go for a small fortune if they come up for sale, usually on the black market.'

'Another dead end, then,' Wen said, tapping her foot.

'Not quite,' Colin replied. 'Father Michael was writing a book about the Knights Templar and their connection with the Temple Church. As he studied in Rome, I'm wondering if he uncovered some new information about The Book. It seems too much of a coincidence that he was bothering Professor Johan.' Colin glanced at the information on the board. 'Especially as the prof's mate in Malta, Dr Dolenz, thought he was on to something important.' Colin pointed to the sentence written at the top.

'In my world, there's no such thing as coincidence, 'said Wen. 'We need to get hold of the priest's laptop.'

'He [15]took it on leave with him, the Grand Master said, and we haven't yet found out where he stayed when he was in Liverpool. If that's where he did stay.'Colin went back to his seat

Cassie looked thoughtful. 'Colin and Ruby, look more closely at places where he may have stayed. Check for feedback on that from the Liverpool team first. When are you searching the Nelsons' house?'

'That's this afternoon, boss.' replied Ruby.

'I don't suppose we've had any sighting of them or their cars, have we?' Wen asked, hopefully.

'Not yet,' said Jake.' But I think I've found their alter egos. Well, his, to be more precise.'

Cassie looked expectant. 'Please share.'

'My friend who works on border patrol ran Nelson's face through his facial-recognition software. Lo and behold...' Jake held up his laptop, showing a photo of a much younger version of Lee Nelson.' Meet Patrick O'Connor, Irish terrorist!'

Cassie congratulated Jake on his breakthrough. Now he could delve more into Patrick O'Connor's background, since that had turned from foggy to merely misty.

'Maybe he just reinvented himself,' suggested Wen, when she and Cassie were back in the office.

'That would explain why the Nelsons' history before they came to Runcorn is blank,' said Cassie. 'But how on earth does an Irish terrorist land a job in a nuclear research facility?'

Wen shrugged.' Doesn't say much for their screening program, does it? I'll give HR a call and ask some pertinent questions. But that will have to be at home, once I've located my baby.' Wen looked into the main office. The two Daisys had reappeared, and the smaller one was getting a lot of attention from her colleagues.

She turned back to Cassie.' Am I a bad mother for just dumping her on someone and not worrying whether she's OK? Or, as my brother said, coming into contact with goodness knows what.'

Cassie smiled.' As far as being a mother goes, you're asking the wrong person. But sooner or later babies have to mix with people to build up their immune system, so I've been told. My mum loves me, but she couldn't wait to get her life back. I think she went back to work the day I started school, but she and Dad have always been there for me.'

'I remember. I thought your dad was going to kill me when you were in hospital.' Wen felt a shiver run down her spine as she recalled Cassie lying outside the office, turning blue through lack of oxygen. 'Right, I'll keep—'

The office phone rang.

'Sorry.' Cassie picked it up. 'DI Rowden. Yes, that's correct. Thank you, I'll be with you directly.'

She replaced the phone in its cradle.' The guy from the Temple Church has arrived to do a formal ID on our murder victim. Have you got time to interview him with me?'

Wen looked out at the main room. 'I'll just have a quick word.' She pointed at DC Pinkman. 'I don't want to take advantage.'

'Daisy.'

DC Pinkman turned, baby in arms. 'Yes, boss?'

'Thank you so much for looking after her. You couldn't manage another half hour, could you? Then I promise I'll relieve you.' Her baby looked at her and smiled, which made Wen feel guilty. 'She seems to like you.' This was said more to herself than to the woman holding her child.

'She's adorable, boss.'

'Not always. But yes, she is cute. Thank you so much. I really must get my childcare sorted: this kind of situation just highlights it.' Wen stroked baby Daisy's face and headed back to Cassie.

'Boss...'

She turned.

'The childcare thing. I might be able to help with that.'

***

Cassie and Wen found the gentleman waiting for them just outside the mortuary.

Wen reached him first. 'Sorry to keep you waiting.'

He stood up. 'Not at all. I know you're busy.' He was about five foot six and slim, completely bald, with no eyebrows or lashes. He wore a smart made-to-measure suit, dark grey, with a white shirt and a dark-grey tie.

'I'm DCI Price, and this is my colleague, DI Rowden.'

'Pleased to meet you. I'm Brian Fletcher, Assistant to the Reader of the Temple. I'm here on behalf of the Grand Master.'

'This way, Mr Fletcher,' said Cassie. 'Or is it Reverend?'

'No, just plain Mr. I am a lawyer, not a member of the clergy.'

'Really? How does that work?' asked Wen.

'The Temple Church was the seat of law in England for many years. It's a historic role: I don't actually do that much.'

Cassie led the way into the viewing room and they approached the covered body. 'Are you ready? I'm afraid he was badly beaten.'

Brian Fletcher replied with a quiet 'Yes.' Cassie nodded to the mortuary assistant, who turned back the sheet.

When Brian looked at the face, he bowed his head.' As far as I can tell, that is the body of Father Michael, though he's in a terrible mess.' He turned away, revolted. 'Who would do that?'

'That's what we're trying to find out,' said Cassie. 'Could you spare a few more minutes, please, for some questions?'

'Of course.' Brian Fletcher followed them to the waiting room and sat down.

'Would you like a drink? 'asked Wen.

He shook his head. 'All coffeed out. If I have any more, I'll start getting jumpy.' He smiled for a second which made a massive difference to his somewhat serious face, then it was gone.

'Did you know Father Michael?' asked Cassie. 'Personally, I mean.'

'Not really. I'd met him, of course, but I didn't know him per se. He seemed a gentle soul. It's hard to equate the body in there with his living spirit.' He sighed. 'It's just too sad.'

'I believe the church will take care of the funeral?' Cassie opened her notebook and picked up her pen.

'Yes, we shall. So if you could let me know when his body may be collected, I'll make the arrangements.'

'Did he have no relatives at all?' Wen asked.

'He does have a brother. I didn't know until I was handed his file last night. It would seem that they were estranged. I did try calling the number in the file but it was discontinued, and there wasn't an address.'

Cassie looked up from her note-taking. 'Did you know he was writing a book?'

'Now, that I did know. Part of my role is education: a teacher, if you like. It occupies only a small part of my time, but the Grand Master did mention a book to me. He asked if I would look over the manuscript when it was complete, to make sure that there were no...' He pondered.' No inconsistencies.'

'Why? Would that matter?' Wen felt that was a strange thing for him to say. What did it mean?

'Conspiracy theories, Detective. We get them all the time. We don't want to have to put bouncers on the door, do we? Otherwise, people might come in and start tearing the place apart, looking for the Holy Grail.' He laughed quietly at this. 'Now, if you will excuse me, I have a train to catch.' He stood up.

'Just one more thing, Mr Fletcher, before you go,' said Wen. 'Have you ever heard of the Book of Sceleratis?'

For a split second, she saw fear. Then it was gone. 'No. Never!'

CHAPTER FOURTEEN

Wen got home just before midday to find Mrs Guess flicking around with her duster.

'How was young missy, then?' she asked as she stroked Daisy's cheek, for which she received a big gummy grin.

'She was fine, Alice. Got a lot of fuss made of her. No trouble at all.' Wen moved past her and put the car seat down on the kitchen table. Her arms were aching, and the baby bag was cutting into her shoulder.

'Your generation of parents will all have bad backs, mark my words. And it's not safe putting her on the table. She might fall off.'

'She's perfectly safe, thank you, Alice. She doesn't have the body strength yet to move that seat.'

'Just saying. I'll go and clean your downstairs loo, then. I know where I'm not wanted.'

'No you don't, 'whispered Wen to Daisy. She wondered yet again why she put up with Mrs Guess, but the answer was always the same: because of Aran. He liked Mrs Guess and she liked him, which was very strange. Also, it hadn't been until Wen was at home all day that she had had anything to do with her. Before then, Mrs Guess had been and gone while Wen was at work.

Her brother came into the kitchen as the clock struck twelve. 'I've made vegetable soup. Do you want some?' he asked, without preamble. A pause.' How did it go?'

'All right, though it gets more and more complicated by the day. We don't seem to be getting anywhere.'

'Not the case – Daisy. And do you want soup or not?'

'Oh. Yes, please. And Daisy was good as gold. In fact, I may have found the answer to our childcare problem,' said Wen, with a smile.

'*Your* problem, not ours. Set the table.'

'Quite.' Wen did as she was told. 'Remember Daisy Pinkman?'

'The woman you named your daughter after? Of course, how could I forget? I only left you for ten minutes. In that time, you came out of your unconscious state and gave your baby a ridiculous name. I mean, *Daisy*?'

'It suits her,' Wen said, defensively. 'Anyway, her younger sister has just lost her job, due to the nursery where she works closing, and—'

'Why?'

'Why what?'

'Why was the nursery closed? Maybe it was because they had really bad staff,' Aran said triumphantly. 'I bet you hadn't thought of that.'

Wen hadn't thought of the whys, more of the wherefores. 'I'll check. The main thing is that she's looking for another job and she's available now. I've invited her round this evening for a chat.'

Aran was ladling hot soup into their bowls. He didn't look up. 'An interview, this evening?'

'A chat, this evening.'

'What time?'

'I said about seven thirty. Her ladyship is usually down by then.'

Aran looked at the space beyond Wen's shoulder and stayed stock still, a sure sign that he was thinking. After a minute or so, he spoke.' Yes, I can accommodate that time frame.'

Wen exhaled, relieved, though she knew the battle wasn't won. Whoever looked after Daisy would need to get on with Aran, as much if not more so than they did with Daisy. If Aran couldn't accept the visitor, it wouldn't matter if the nanny was Mary Poppins herself: she wouldn't do.

'I'm off,' said Alice Guess, buttoning her coat. 'Bye, Aran love, bye Daisy.' And one more gruff 'bye' for Wen.

***

Ruby and Colin gowned up in SOCO clothes and entered what was now known as the O'Connors' house in Runcorn. It was a fairly nondescript new semi with clean lines, a nice kitchen-diner overlooking a rectangular garden, fitted wardrobes upstairs, and no character at all.

'I'd have thought this couple's earnings would warrant a more impressive house than this,' said Ruby as she opened and closed cupboards in the kitchen, taking out tins and packets to investigate for anything unusual.

'I think they just wanted a place to live that wouldn't draw attention. I mean, look around you. No pictures or knickknacks: it's like a short-term rental. Didn't he say they had been here five years? It doesn't feel like that.' Colin put his hands on his hips and blew at a hair that had escaped from his hood and was tickling his nose.

'Got to agree with you, Col. No one had a subscription to *Homes Beautiful* at this dwelling.'

A uniformed officer looked into the room. 'Sorry, Sarge. A man here wants a word.'

Colin went outside and saw a man who looked just like an estate agent. 'Can I help you sir?'

'I hope so. My name is Paul Bennet. I'm an estate agent, from Mood and Bennet.'

Colin smiled: got it in one. 'And what can I do for you, Mr Bennet?'

'I've been instructed to put this property on the market, but you seem a bit busy at the moment.'

'Yes, we are. Can I ask who gave you these instructions?'

'A large property company, based in London.'

'And what is this company called?'

'They have properties all over the UK, apparently. Grosvenor Investments.'

'That's interesting. Can you give me your card, please? I may need to speak to you further.'

***

Daisy was napping and Wen knew it wouldn't last long, so she opened her laptop and brought up the website of Daresbury Laboratory, on the edge of Runcorn and Warrington. It had opened in 1962, and employed approximately three hundred staff at present.

She found the HR department's phone number in the case file and called. It rang for a considerable amount of time before someone answered. 'Human Resources, Karen speaking. How can I help?'

'Hello. My name is Detective Chief Inspector Price from Cheshire Serious Crime Squad. I'd like to speak to someone about one of your employees, a Mr Lee Nelson.'

'I'll just put you through to our head of section.' Wen didn't even get a chance to thank the woman before piped music came at her through the phone.

Wen was left on hold for almost ten minutes. She was just about to hang up and redial when the music cut off and a sharp male voice spoke. 'Sorry to keep you waiting. What is it you want, exactly?'

'Hi. I just want some information about a Lee Nelson who works for you.'

'I'm sorry, but you have been misinformed. We have no one of that name working here.' The line went dead.

***

Jake was doing what he did best: poking into other people's lives. It was like Big Brother, only real. The best part of Jake's work involved getting information on others: information that would see him arrested if he didn't work for the police. Even a straightforward search on the internet could lead down many rabbit holes.

Patrick O'Connor had been under the scrutiny of various organisations for years, ever since his undergraduate days at the University of Oxford. He had read physics, and had had a reputation for being very outspoken about the situation in the Republic of Ireland. He had written about Sinn Fein for a college rag, arguing that the party should have been more aggressive in their campaign for the people's rights.

He graduated with a double first, then disappeared. He was next seen in the USA, where he was arrested for planning to make a bomb. And that was the end of the trail, as far as Jake could see.

He tried another website, and came up with some family history. Patrick's mother, Siobhan, had died of cancer when Patrick was only five. His father, also called Patrick, was heavily into politics, and had worked for Sinn Fein as a political analyst.

Jake read on, and did a double take. He looked up from his computer and saw an almost empty office. 'Damn!' He went over to Ruby's desk and scanned the files sitting on it.

'Hey, laughing boy, what are you doing at my desk?'

Jake jumped. 'Bloody hell, Ruby, why can't you wear clicky heels like all the other women in the office?' He paused to get his breath back. 'You weren't out long.'

'No, there wasn't anything much to see. I left Colin to oversee the rest of the operation and headed back.'

Jake smiled. Anyone who didn't know the office dynamics would have presumed that Ruby was Colin's boss.

'Anyway, don't change the subject.' Ruby took off her jacket and hung it on the back of her chair. 'What are you up to?'

'Can you tell me what the murdered priest's full name was? I've only ever heard him referred to as Father Michael.'

'Couldn't say.' Ruby sat down and pressed a few keys.' It's here somewhere. Here we go. Father Michael O'Connor.'

Jake smiled. 'Come and look at this.'

'But I've only just sat down!' Ruby sighed, but followed him.

Jake dismissed his screensaver and showed Ruby what had made him sit up straight a few moments ago.

'OMG' said Ruby. 'That's Patrick O'Connor.' She peered at the writing under the photo.'Patrick O'Connor shares his acceptance to Oxford.' she read. '"We are so proud," said his younger brother, Michael.'

She turned to Jake. 'They're brothers?'

'Yes, Ruby. They're brothers.'

'His brother?' said Wen, clutching the phone to her ear. 'Are we sure? I mean, O'Connor must be a common name in Ireland.'

'Yes,' said Cassie. 'Jake found an old picture of them together online. Too much of a coincidence?'

'With the body found so close to the brother's house? What do you think?'

'I think we need to up our game to find this man and his wife. They could have some of the answers.'

'I agree. 'The doorbell rang. 'Sorry, Cassie, I have to go. I'll schedule a Zoom meeting tomorrow to discuss this further. I won't be able to get into the office. Speak soon.'

She hung up and looked at her watch. Ten past seven. 'She's early,' Wen said to herself. She didn't mind, but Aran would be put out.

Wen opened the front door to a younger version of Daisy Pinkman, wearing a crisp white blouse and blue trousers, and carrying a blue jacket. 'Sorry I'm early,' she said. 'I had to come across Warrington, and you know how bad the traffic can be.' She sounded nervous, but then she was coming into the unknown.

'Not a problem, better early than late.' Wen smiled at her. 'Come in. Rose, isn't it?'

'Yes.' She was wiping her feet on the doormat as Aran came downstairs.

Wen looked up at her brother, who had stopped three stairs from the hallway. 'Aran, this is Rose Pinkman, Daisy's sister.'

Aran gave her a cursory look. 'You're early.'

'Yes, we've covered that. Rose, this is my brother, Aran. Shall we go into the sitting room?' Wen led the way, and Aran followed Rose. He was holding a large notebook and a pen, which made Wen apprehensive.

They all sat down in a room which Wen and Aran barely used. It was too formal for Wen's liking. She and Aran tended to congregate in the large kitchen-diner, with its old comfy settees and battered kitchen table.

'I didn't hear your car pull up,' said Wen.

'Oh, I parked just down the road and walked here,' Rose explained. 'I must say, this is a lovely house.'

'You've only seen this room,' Aran pointed out.' You might hate the rest of the place.'

Rose looked put out.' I meant from the outside.'

Aran considered this, then nodded.' Yes, I suppose it is pleasing to the eye.'

'Rose, would you like a coffee or a tea before we start?' asked Wen.

'I'm fine, thanks.' She put her jacket beside her on the settee.

'Is it just you and Daisy? No other brothers or sisters?' Wen asked, to try and lighten the tense atmosphere.

'I have another sister, between me and Daisy. Heather.'

'Your parents must love gardening,' Aran said, opening his notebook. Wen's heart dropped several feet. 'Now, can we see your qualifications, your references, and places that you have worked so far?'

Daisy opened her bag and retrieved a manila folder which she passed to Aran.

'While I scrutinise these, Wen, you may continue with the interview.'

Rose was looking most uncomfortable, and Wen feared she might flee at any second. 'Rose, your last job came to an end. That must have been very disappointing.'

'Er, yes. I was working at a nursery in Widnes, and I'd only been there six months when Covid struck. The owner became ill, and then there were money issues. We struggled along, but finally it had to close. That was my first job as a nursery nurse. Before I went to college to train, I worked in the family business.' She looked down. 'A flower shop.'

Aran smiled.' That explains it.'

'I'm sorry, but we like our names. And your niece is named after my sister,' Rose said, sounding not far from crying.

'I was stating a fact,' said Aran.' Our parents were *Lord of the Rings* fanatics. Hence Aragorn' – he pointed to himself –' and Arwen.' He pointed at Wen.

A bright smile lit up Rose's face. 'Really? Oh, that's so cool! I love *The Lord of the Rings*. I've read the books so many times, and of course there are the films! Not as good as the books, in my opinion, but pretty spectacular.'

That was it. Aran and Rose chatted about their favourite characters and the actors who played them, and Wen sat and listened.

An hour later, Rose left, having been offered the job of Daisy's nanny on a trial basis, starting in three days' time.

'I take it you approve,' said Wen, as she waved the young woman goodbye.

'We will see,' said Aran. 'But she will do for now.'

CHAPTER FIFTEEN

Wen was still in her pyjamas when her phone rang. She had had another bad night with Daisy. She wasn't ill: she just didn't want to sleep when it was dark and everyone else was tired. She wanted to play.

'Hello, Cassie,' she said, sounding brighter than she felt.

'Sorry to bother you, but you're needed in the office.'

'When?'

'Now. Or at least, as soon as you can get here. It's urgent, or I wouldn't bother you.'

This all sounded very mysterious, but the tone of Cassie's voice told Wen that it couldn't wait.

'All right, but I may have to bring Daisy with me. I'll ask Aran, but he hates things being dropped on him without warning.'

'OK. And again, I'm sorry.'

'See you in about forty minutes.' Wen hung up, then picked up her daughter's Moses basket and took her to the bathroom.

It was almost an hour later when Wen entered the squad room. The swing bridge in Stockton Heath had been closed to traffic for several minutes to allow a boat to go through.

'No baby?' Cassie asked.

'She's with her very disgruntled uncle. On the upside, I have a nanny starting in two days.' Wen took off her coat and threw it on an empty chair. 'What's so urgent?'

'Come into the office,' Cassie said quietly. 'A spook wants to talk to us.' Of all the things Wen had considered on her drive into the centre of Warrington, that hadn't been anywhere near the top of her list.

They entered and Cassie carefully closed the door behind her. Sitting in Cassie's seat and holding a large mug of coffee was a red-haired man, wearing a dark-blue suit and a white shirt with the top button undone. The outfit seemed to suggest he was relaxed, down with the team, a friend. It didn't work.

Cassie introduced Wen. He stood up, leaned across the desk and shook her hand. His grip was warm and firm. 'Hi I'm James.'

Cassie sat down and Wen took the seat next to her. 'Wen, this is Mr Brand. He works for—'

'Security services,' said James. He walked around the desk and sat on the edge near the detectives. Up close, he had the longest eyelashes Wen had ever seen on a man. 'I'm sorry to bring you in on your day off, Detective Chief Inspector, but the matter is of some importance.'

'I'm very part-time at the moment, Mr Brand, so it's not actually my day off. I come into the office when needed and work from home the rest of the time.'

'Do call me James, please.'

Wen looked at Cassie and they both smiled.

'Yes, my name is somewhat unfortunate, given my line of work. But I don't like Jimmy or Jim, so I just have to put up with the jokes.'

Wen decided to cut to the chase. 'What can we do for the security services then, James?'

As James perched on the desk, one foot on the floor and his arms across his lap, Wen noticed his nails. He was clearly no stranger to the manicurist's table. 'The case you are currently working on overlaps with one of our operations. I can't tell you very much, and I need you both to sign this before we go any further.' He turned slightly, picked up two sheets of paper, and handed one to each of them.

'Official Secrets Act?' Wen looked up at him.' Really?'

'Yes, really. Don't worry, it's a formality. You won't end up in the Tower.' He paused.' Hopefully, 'he added, and smiled.

The two detectives read, signed, and handed back the papers. He checked them and placed them on the desk at his side. 'The first time I had to sign one of these, I was doing unemployment statistics for the Department of Employment. Ah, those were the days. Anyhow, back to business.'

'Please,' said Wen, uneasy at all this cloak-and-dagger talk.

'Patrick O'Connor is one of ours, so please stop looking into his background and trying to find him. In fact, forget all about him.'

'One of ours?' Cassie frowned. 'What does that mean?'

'That information is need-to-know only. And I'm afraid you don't need to know.'

'What?!' cried Wen. 'He's a key witness for his brother's brutal murder.'

'But he didn't kill his brother and he doesn't know who did. He shouldn't have phoned the police at all when he came across the body: that was a mistake. Michael was staying with him and his wife. He shouldn't even have known where Patrick lived, but they had stayed in touch. Another error. Michael turned up desperate a few nights before the murder, begging for help. He said he was being followed and Patrick allowed him in. He shouldn't have. Michael went out the second night he was with them and didn't come back.'

'Was this murder related to whatever you're working on?' Cassie asked.

James Brand shook his head very slowly. 'We don't think so. But we've had to relocate Patrick and his wife and delete his history. Years of work down the drain.' He stood up and began putting things in his briefcase.

'That's it?' said Wen, staring. 'That's all you're going to say?'

He smiled again and went to the door. As he passed, Wen caught a hint of citrusy cologne. 'Good luck with your enquiries, ladies,' he said, and left.

'What the hell!' Wen looked at her colleague. 'That's our strongest lead up in smoke.'

'Do you think Patrick was always working for them?' asked Cassie. 'Was he recruited at Oxford, or was he turned?'

'I have no idea, and I don't suppose we'll ever know. What do we tell the team?' Wen asked.

'As much as we can, which isn't much at all. We've been told by a higher authority not to go there,' Cassie said bitterly.

'They won't like it.'

'*I* don't like it, 'said Cassie, 'but there's sod all we can do about it.'

***

Cassie faced the team briefing without Wen, who had gone home to relieve Aran.

'What do you mean, they've been removed from our enquiries?' asked Colin, when he had recovered himself enough to speak.

'Exactly that. Ask me no questions and I'll tell you no lies.'

'It was that suit, wasn't it?' Colin wasn't going to let this go easily.

'Sergeant Briggs, leave it. I don't like this either, but there's nothing we can do about it. We need to press on with any other leads we have. Ruby, any trace of the priest's laptop? We've been told it wasn't at his place of residence, so presumably he brought it with him.'

'Sorry, boss, but there was no sign of it at the O'Connors' house. In fact, there was nothing to show that Father Michael had ever been there.'

'Maybe that's why they tortured him and stripped him,' Colin said thoughtfully. 'He could have had files on a pen drive. They were probably searching his clothes.'

'I wonder...'Cassie tapped her pen on her teeth, a habit which drove Ruby mad. 'Ruby and Colin, I want you to look at the CCTV of Michael's meeting with the professor again. Watch it very carefully.'

'Because he might have passed it to the prof?' said Colin, and smiled.

'The DCI and I are having a Zoom meeting with Liverpool and Malta again in the morning. We'll throw a few ideas around and see where that gets us.'

'Now we know why he was in bits,' Ruby said quietly. 'Imagine finding your own brother like that.'

***

At home, Wen fed Daisy, who was bright and cheerful after her 'long nap,' as Aran put it. 'She was no trouble at all,' he said, before going upstairs to his rooms.

'I'm sure you weren't,' Wen said to her grinning daughter, 'but we've got to get this night and day thing sorted out, Daisy. I'm so tired, and I've got work to do.'

Daisy smiled, then burped.

Wen put the infant over her shoulder and rubbed her back gently, trying to encourage trapped wind out. 'You think it's funny, do you? It's a good job I love you. I wonder what your dad would have thought of you.'

Daisy gurgled.

'You're right: he would have adored you.' Wen felt the sting of tears as she rocked Daisy on her shoulder and as the tiny head grew heavier. She lay back against the settee, and soon both mother and baby were asleep.

The doorbell rang and Wen jumped, but Daisy just grunted. Wen was able to get up and carefully put Daisy in her pram, which had taken up residence in the kitchen with further baby paraphernalia.

The doorbell rang a second time. Wen winced as she went to answer it. Had it always sounded that harsh?

The tall shadow behind the frosted glass could only be one person. Wen opened the door. 'John! What are you doing here?'

'Sorry, is it a bad time?' He smiled, and Wen tried not to frown at what she felt was his unnecessarily loud voice. 'You look tired.'

'Thank you for that.'

'Well, you do. Small baby, working again. Not really surprising that you look a bit discombobulated.'

'Discombobulated? Have you been doing the *Times* crossword again?' She stepped aside to allow John in and glanced at herself in the hall mirror. Her make-up, such as it was, had slipped down her face and her hair was a mess. Maybe she should get it cut short. Jeff had loved her long hair, but he wasn't there to see it any more.

'Where shall I go?' John asked.

Wen put her finger to her lips.' Shh, Daisy's asleep in the kitchen. Let's go into the sitting room. Do you want a drink?' She hoped he would say no. Making coffee or tea would probably disturb her sleeping child.

'No, I'm fine.'

'What are you doing here? Not that it isn't nice to see you.'

'I was just passing, and I—'

Wen's eyes narrowed. 'Just passing to go where?'

'To gun club.'

'Gun club? I didn't know you liked guns.'

'Why should you? Anyway, I've been thinking about your case, and I had an idea.'

'Good, because we're running out of those very quickly.' Wen yawned. 'Sorry, 'she said, then saw John's smile. 'What?'

'I've never seen you look anything but professional. Smart clothes, perfect hair and make-up.'

'Not even when you came to see me in hospital?'

John flushed. 'How do you know about that? Did one of the team tell you?'

'Aran did.'

'Aran. Of course.'

'He saw you leaving a few times when he was coming in. But once I started to improve, you stopped visiting.'

'I just wanted to make sure you were out of danger.' He looked down for a moment, then smiled at her. 'So, do you want to know my theory?'

***

Colin and Ruby watched, then rewatched the small amount of CCTV they had of the two victims together, but no matter how hard they looked, they couldn't see any objects being handed over.

'Someone needs to go back to the people the DI interviewed in Liverpool,' said Colin. 'They may have noticed something.'

'Definitely the lady in the cafe and the secretary,' said Ruby. 'They were the only people who actually saw Father Michael. Apart from the prof, that is.' Ruby thought for a moment. 'Maybe he hid it in the professor's office?'

'It's worth a look, but the Liverpool team needs to do that. You know what it'll be like if we step on their toes.'

'Would a joint interview be acceptable?' Ruby put her head on one side and smiled.

'I'll have a word with the boss.' Colin studied his colleague. She might get on his nerves at times, but she was very good at her job. 'Ruby, I never really asked you about your sergeant's exam. I expected you'd pass and I'd fail.'

Ruby sighed. ' I'd had a bereavement the day before. My head was all over the place.'

'Oh no. I thought you looked upset, but I just thought you'd found the exam tough. I'm so sorry. Was it someone close?'

'Yes. My best friend.'

'Oh, Ruby. How old was – she? He?'

'He was eighteen.'

'God, that's so young.'

Ruby looked puzzled. 'Actually, that's a grand age for a cat.'

'A *cat*? You're talking about a cat?'

'Yes, I am.' Ruby scowled. 'You don't do pets, do you, Colin, or you would understand.'

'I don't have time for a dog and cats make me sneeze. So you failed your sergeant's exam because your cat died?' Colin was about to laugh when he saw a tear run down Ruby's cheek. She sprang up and hurried out.

Jake came over to Colin's desk. 'What have you done now?'

'Her cat died. I didn't know.'

'Oh yes, Mr Holmes.'

'Mr Holmes?' Colin chuckled. 'This gets better and better. Anyway, how come you know the name of Ruby's cat?'

'We go for a drink now and again. She's a good listener, she isn't scared of offending me, and she calls a spade a shovel.'

'Oh, I see,' said Colin, raising his eyebrows.

'I don't think you do. We're friends. Friends who work together.'

Colin grinned. 'If you say so.'

'I do. But Ruby loved that cat. She said it made all the difference when you had a pet waiting for you at home, even if it was just to be fed.'

'I suppose.' Colin felt guilty for making Ruby cry.

'Anyway, back to work,' said Jake. 'I thought you might find this interesting.' He handed Colin a piece of paper. 'This is a copy of a page from the World Museum's visitors' book. People have to sign in if they don't have a museum pass for the staff-only area. One of the people interviewed by our DI signed in on the day the priest visited the professor, but there's nothing about that in their statement. Can you spot who?'

CHAPTER SIXTEEN

The following morning, Wen and Cassie were huddled around a laptop in the office, waiting for others to join the Zoom meeting with Liverpool and Malta.

'John had a good point, though,' said Wen. 'We've been assuming that because the two murders in the UK are linked, they were committed by the same person or group. But there's more of a link between the Liverpool case and the murder in Malta: the MO is the same. The priest's murder was completely different.' Wen bit into a biscuit, vowing yet again to improve her diet. Apart from the food Aran prepared, she ate mostly junk.

Brendan Wild suddenly appeared on screen.' Good morning, ladies, 'he said, with a sunny smile.

'Good morning, DCI Wild,' said Cassie.

'Brendan, please. How are things at your end?'

Wen and Cassie told him that part of their investigation had stalled, and why. 'Bloody spies,' said DCI Wild, shaking his head. 'They say jump and we say how high.'

Just then Luca joined them from his office in Malta. 'What have I missed? Spies? This all sounds very James Bond.'

'James Brand, actually, Luca,' said Cassie.' But yes, it was a bit 007.'

They each gave a summary of where they were up to in their investigations. First, DCI Wild said he had nothing new to add. Then Wen and Cassie told the group about the idea John had come up with. 'The murders may be part of the same case, but committed by different people who aren't acting together,' said Wen.

'That makes sense,' said Luca, and sipped his coffee.' We have no idea how many factions are after this manuscript, or why. All I know is that no one is talking to us about the Knights Templar or any other secret society.' He smiled. 'Which is why they are still secret societies!'

'Just for a moment, let's allow our police imaginations to run free,' said Wen.

Wild frowned. 'In what way?'

'Let's think of all the reasons why anyone would want to get their hands on the Book of Sceleratis. I mean, they want it so badly that they've killed for it.'

'It's worth a small fortune,' said Cassie.

'It could shape a career,' added Wild.

'Someone wants to show the world what it says,' said Luca.

'Or someone wants to make sure that it's never seen again.' Ideas began to shift in Wen's brain as she said this.

'Brendan, would it be OK if two of our detectives called on Professor Gryfinn? I'm not sure he's been totally honest with us.' Cassie had informed her that he had entered the museum's staff-only area on the day when the priest had visited Professor Johan, but the professor had not declared this to the police.

'I'd love to know how he managed that without being seen on any of the CCTV footage,' said DCI Wild. 'We know the secretary saw the priest in the office, but she didn't mention seeing Gryfinn.'

'She could be lying,' said Luca. 'Or perhaps she wasn't in the office when Professor Gryfinn called.'

'Right.' Wild sat back in his chair.' You send your detectives to visit Gryfinn, and my guys will talk to Susan and Jessica again. Let's see if we get anywhere with a two-pronged attack.'

The Zoom meeting ended and Cassie studied Wen. 'Have you had an idea?'

'Yes. It's too ridiculous to even contemplate, but here I am doing just that.'

'Can you share?'

'Not yet, but soon. I just need to talk to a few more people first. That is, if they'll talk to me.'

***

'Why did you phone him?' Ruby asked, between mouthfuls of

dried fruit.

'Because it's a long way to go to find he's not at home,' Colin replied, changing gear. They were on their way to Liverpool to interview Professor Gryfinn, who lived in the highly sought-after area of Aigburth.

'True. But I do like the element of surprise, don't you?' said Ruby, with a smile. 'The bewildered look on their faces when they open the door and see the police standing there. The worry about what their neighbours will think.' She popped a piece of banana into her mouth.

'Wouldn't you prefer fresh fruit to that dehydrated stuff?' Colin knew Ruby was always on a diet, and he also knew just how many calories were hidden in so-called healthy snacks, only because his mum worked for a weight loss company.

'I see it this way, Col.' She held up the bag.' This is better than eating chocolate, which is what I really want. If I keep a bag of dried fruit in my drawer, it stops me going to the vending machine. And who knew we wouldn't have time for lunch today?'

She offered the pack to Colin, who shook his head.' No thanks, Ruby.'

'Turn left in one hundred yards,' commanded the satnav.

Colin glanced at Ruby.' I haven't said sorry about the other day.'

'Sorry for what?'

'About your cat, um, Mr Holmes.' Colin coughed. 'You're right that I don't do pets, but I should do sympathy, and I wasn't very nice about it.'

Ruby said nothing for a moment.' It's OK. I know a lot of people think it's stupid to get so upset about an animal, but Mr Holmes was so much more than that. To me, anyhow.'

'Will you get another one? Another cat, I mean?'

'Yes, when the time is right. I might even get an adult cat that needs a good home.'

'Not a kitten, then? 'Colin had always thought that people had cats from the tiny cute age.

'Kittens take a lot of looking after at first. An adult cat who's litter trained and happy to be left all day is probably a better fit for me right now.'

'Next right, and you have reached your destination.'

The car pulled up a few minutes later outside a rather grand terraced house built of sandstone.

'Nice,' said Ruby, as she got out of the car. Colin followed her up the path. She had already rung the bell before he reached her.

There was no answer.

She rang again, and also knocked.

Nothing.

'Did you tell him when we'd be coming?' Ruby bent down to look through the letterbox.

'I said about two,' said Colin, looking at his watch. 'It's half past, but we're not *that* late. I don't drive as fast as you, Rubes. I'll go round the back.' Colin walked round the side of the house while Ruby tried the door again.

He had been gone only a minute or two, but Ruby was already tired of waiting. 'Where has he got to?' she muttered, and went in search of her partner.

The back gate was unfastened, and Ruby shouted to Colin as she pushed it open, revealing a long, beautifully manicured garden. But something felt wrong. 'Colin!' she called again, hearing the panic in her voice. She felt a shiver of fear run the full length of her spine.

As she turned the corner of the house, she saw Colin lying on the ground about five feet away, his hair a bloody mess. She gasped, and was frozen to the spot. She willed her legs to move, to run to him.

But before she could reach Colin, something struck the back of her head. As Ruby fell onto the patio and heard a sickening crunch, her only thought was *Please don't let him be dead...*

***

'My name is Detective Chief Inspector Price from Cheshire

Serious Crime Squad. Is Leonard Deed available, please? I'd like to speak to him about a current investigation concerning a member of your clergy.'

'One moment, please.'

Wen tapped her fingers on the table, fully expecting to be told that the Grand Master was unavailable and she would need to make an appointment for a call. She was thoroughly taken aback when a smooth voice said, 'Detective Chief Inspector, how can I help you?'

'Oh, um, thank you, Mr, er, Reverend…'

'Just call me Leo, please.'

'Right. Thank you, Leo. I didn't think I would get put straight through.'

'I have nothing planned that can't wait. Your work, your efforts to bring the murderer of one of my priests to justice, takes precedence over more mundane matters.'

'Er, yes, indeed.'

'I rather hope you're calling to inform me that we can have Father Michael back, so that we may lay his body to rest.'

'Sorry, not yet. I will try to find out how much longer the coroner needs to, um, keep him, and get back to you. But today I wanted to, well, ask for your opinion on the background surrounding his death.' Wen tried not to sound as if she was about to grill a suspect.

'Of course. Anything I can do to help.'

'We are currently investigating four linked murders: two on our patch, including Father Michael, one in Liverpool, and one in Malta.'

Wen heard an intake of breath on the other end of the line. 'Goodness. This is all very mysterious, Detective Chief Inspector, but I don't see how I am in a position to help.'

'Wen, please. You may not be able to help, Leo, but I don't know who else to turn to.' She hoped that pleading might convey just how desperate she was.

'Then ask away, Wen, and I will do my best to help in any way I can.'

Wen remembered what Ruby had said about the Grand Master's voice. It was indeed rich and comforting. 'The first three murders have one thing in common, Leo: the Book of Sceleratis. The first murder took place when a copy was stolen in transit to a Professor Johan. The professor was stabbed to death just when he thought he had a lead on the original artefact. His colleague in Malta, with whom he was working on this theory, was murdered in the same way, and at the same time.' She let that information settle for a moment. 'We believe Father Michael went to Liverpool to warn off Professor Johan. We have proof that they met. And the next day, they were both dead.'

The line was quiet. Wen wondered if she had asked the wrong person the wrong questions. When Leo did speak, it was slow and considered.

'The Book of Sceleratis is a story, like many ancient artefacts. A story of faith. It is not as famous as some, because no one apart from a few learned academics knows of its existence.'

'So it exists?'

'It probably *has* existed. But does it still? I doubt that very much.' He sounded sad.

'You told my detectives when they came to see you that it contained the words of Jesus Christ. We were led to believe by Professor Johan that the book held the writings of the first Grand Master of The Knights Templar.'

'That story is told to protect what the book actually is, or is supposed to be. Jesus's last will and testament, if you like, written before his crucifixion.'

'And eventually, this ended up in the protection of the Knights Templar?'

'I'm impressed Wen. You have done your homework. The story goes that the scroll was given to one of the twelve disciples. Others speculate that Jesus gave it to Mary Magdalene for safekeeping.'

'And the truth?'

'And the truth is that no one knows.' The Grand Master took a deep breath.' If it were true, imagine reading the actual word of

God. It would be more important than the Dead Sea Scrolls or the Ten Commandments.'

Wen took her time asking the next question.' Leo, is there anyone, or any group, who would be prepared to kill to make sure that no one ever sees it?'

A pause. 'I can't think why. Such a manuscript could give many people hope and faith.'

'I can't equate that with the deaths we have seen since the copy of this book re-emerged,' said Wen. 'I suspect that someone, or something, doesn't want this manuscript ever to be made public.'

'Like who? Like what? 'asked Leo.

'Like the Church.'

CHAPTER SEVENTEEN

Cassie ran down a corridor in the Royal Liverpool University Hospital, looking for the A&E department. She had driven all the way from Warrington on blues and twos. However, there was nowhere to park near A&E, even with her police ID in the window, so she had had to leave her car at the car park across the road, and now she was completely lost.

'Excuse me!' she shouted at a man in scrubs. 'A&E?'

'Down there, turn left,' he said, without breaking stride.

In the A&E reception, she saw DCI Wild talking to some uniformed officers, all with cups in their hands. 'Brendan!'

'Cassie, calm down.' He took her arm. 'It's OK.'

'What happened? Where are they? How are they?'

'Come in here.' Wild guided her into a relatives' room and shut the door. 'DS Braggs—'

'Briggs.'

'Briggs is in theatre. He had a brain bleed, so they're sorting that out. Your female detective…'

'Ruby Wall.'

'Yes, sorry. Ruby is pretty bashed up, but it's nothing life-threatening. It appears that they interrupted a burglary. Wrong time wrong place, for all concerned.'

'Well, it will be for the scumbag who bashed my officers when I get hold of them. Any idea who it was?'

'No, but there have been a number of break-ins in that area lately. We have a team on it.'

'What about Gryfinn? He knew they were coming to see him.'

'Vanished.'

'Vanished? What do you mean, vanished?' Cassie could feel herself getting more and more agitated.

'He wasn't in the house. His car has gone, and his phone is switched off. Vanished!'

Cassie shook her head. 'I don't believe this. My officers make arrangements to go and interview a man and just happen to walk in on a local burglar who beats the living shit out of them.'

'Look, Cassie, I know this is confusing, but I'm just telling you what we actually know at this point in time. There might be more to it, but this is what we have to work on for now.'

'More to it? You think?'

'Please, DI Rowden, don't forget which of us is the senior officer and whose patch you're on.' He was just about to say something else when a man in blue surgical scrubs came in.

'Hi. I'm Mr Long, consultant neurosurgeon. Hello again, DCI Wild. I've just operated on Colin Briggs.' He looked at Cassie. 'Are you his wife?'

'No, I'm his senior officer. Colin is one of my police officers. How is he?'

'He's OK. We've stopped the bleed and he's now in ICU. Hopefully, he will make a good recovery.'

Cassie rubbed the bridge of her nose. 'Hopefully?'

'Yes. All the signs are good, but with a brain injury we can never be a hundred per cent sure that the person will be quite the same as they were before. It's just time and observation for now.'

'Thank you.' Cassie knew all too well what an assault on the brain could cause. 'How is Ruby Wall, please?'

'She isn't one of my patients, but I'll enquire.' He disappeared, and left the pair avoiding each other's gaze.

Cassie could bear it no longer. 'I'm sorry, DCI Wild. It's just that none of this makes sense.'

'I know. But we'll get to the bottom of it eventually.'

It seemed like hours, but it was probably about twenty minutes later when a woman appeared, also in scrubs. Cassie wondered if doctors wore white coats any more. 'Are you Ruby's relatives?' she asked, smiling.

The pair explained their connection again. 'Right. Well, Ruby will need surgery, but she's stable at the moment. She has a fractured eye socket and cheekbone, and she has lost a few teeth. We'll have to pin the cheekbone, but I'm hoping that once the swelling from the eye injury goes down it will be fine. Would you like to see her?'

'Yes, please.' Cassie moved forward, then turned to Wild. 'I'll be in touch later.'

'We'll take a short statement from Ruby after you've seen her, and Colin tomorrow, if he's fit,' he replied.

She followed the doctor, who led her to a cubicle in A&E. As she drew back the curtain, Cassie had to stop herself from putting her hand to her mouth.

Ruby's face was bright red with tinges of blue. The left side of her face was twice the size of the right, and her left eyelid was swollen closed.

'Oh, Ruby.'

'Hi, boss,' she said in a whisper. 'Can't really talk. Hurts.' Her words were slurred, but Cassie didn't know if this was due to her injuries or her medication.

'Don't even try. I'll contact your mum and dad and let them know.'

'How is...' Ruby winced.

'Colin?'

Ruby nodded.

'He's doing OK. He's recovering from an op to stop a brain bleed.' Ruby's mouth opened. 'But he's doing well, so don't you worry.' Cassie paused. 'Wild's lot want to interview you, but I don't think you're up to it.'

Ruby shook her head, very slowly.

'Right. I'll have a word, then get back to the office.' She handed Ruby her notebook and a pen. 'Write down anything you remember that might be important, and also anything you need. If your mum can't bring those things, I'll come back this evening with them. I'll go and speak to the DCI, then pop back for your list.'

Ruby nodded, tears streaming down one side of her face. Was it because of the pain, or was it relief that she and Colin were still alive? Cassie squeezed her hand. 'It will be all right, Ruby, I promise.'

***

After Cassie had got an update on Colin's condition, she phoned Jake. 'I need phone numbers for Ruby's and Colin's next of kin. I know I should go through HR, but I need them now.'

'On it. Just hang on a mo. How are they, Cassie?' Jake asked as he tapped away on his keyboard.

'Stable. Ruby's face is a mess. Colin's still unconscious, but his op went well.'

'Op? What op?'

'He had a bleed on his brain, but they're confident he's going to be OK.' It was a white lie, really, she thought. After all, the doctor had said Colin's outcome looked good.

'Right. I'll send you the information, boss.'

'Thanks, Jake.'

'Cassie…can I visit Ruby?'

Cassie wondered why Jake was so keen. 'Um, maybe leave it a day or two, Jake. Then I'm sure she'll be pleased to see you.'

After notifying the officers' families and making sure they could get to the hospital, Cassie headed straight to see Wen, who was both surprised and shaken by her DI's news.

'Drink this, and tell me what happened.' Wen handed her DI a large glass of wine, her heart going out to her. This was the first time Cassie had had to deal with her officers being injured in the line of duty.

Cassie looked at the glass, then away. 'I can't drink that, Wen, I'm driving.'

'You can either get a taxi or stay the night. God knows we have enough rooms.'

Cassie didn't need asking twice; she accepted the glass and swallowed half its contents in one go. 'Thank you. Do you think all police officers are doomed to become alcoholics?'

Wen laughed.' No, but I think any stressful job can lead to self-medicating if you're not careful. It won't happen in this house though. Aran disapproves of me drinking. He's my sober companion, even if I don't need one.'

Wen topped up Cassie's glass, then poured a smaller one for herself. 'This measure is because Daisy will get me up at three in the morning.' She held the glass to the light and inspected it. 'It's strange – babies change your life in so many ways I hadn't even considered.'

'But you wouldn't be without her?'

'I can't even remember what I did with my time before Daisy. But she's a little miracle. I know it won't be easy, but it'll be worth it.'

'Here's to Daisy.' Cassie held her glass up and they clinked a toast.

'That's the closest I've got to wetting the baby's head,' said Wen, as she sipped her drink. 'Now, tell me all.'

Cassie had burst into Wen's quiet evening with what had happened tumbling out of her mouth. Now they sat together, and she told Wen as much as she knew.

'Colin's stable,' reiterated Wen, 'and Ruby will be OK in time. Let's be grateful for that.'

'But I don't agree with Wild. He reckons they just happened to interrupt a burglar, and oh, by the way, Gryfinn has gone.'

'You don't think much of Brendan Wild, do you?'

Cassie sipped her wine, considering her reply. 'I don't trust him,' she said, slowly.

'Why not?'

'I can't tell you, because I'm not sure myself. His interview technique leaves a lot to be desired, and who else knew that Colin and Ruby were visiting Gryfinn this afternoon?'

'If he briefed his team, as we do, lots of people would know.' Wen wanted Cassie to think logically, but she knew from experience that when it came to the welfare of your officers, logic often went out of the window. 'So, what do you think?'

Cassie took another sip of her drink. 'This might be the wine talking, or the comedown from the adrenaline, but…'

'But?'

'I think Gryfinn has either run away because he's up to his

neck in all this, or he's been taken. The so-called robbers could have been there to snatch Gryfinn before we reached him, but they weren't quick enough.'

Wen blew out her cheeks.' That's a theory, all right. But one of our squad could be the informer.'

'No! Never!'

'Don't forget, not many people knew the book was being taken to Liverpool that day, or which way we were going.'

'But we investigated that and came up with nothing.'

'Just because we didn't come up with any leads, Cassie, that doesn't mean there wasn't a leak.'

'Maybe. Anyway, how did you get on with your idea?' Cassie asked.

'I spoke to the Grand Master but he wasn't that helpful, especially when I asked if the church could be involved in keeping The Book hidden.'

'Which church? There are so many.'

'I was thinking the Church of England or the Roman Catholic Church.'

'No wonder he wasn't helpful.'

'Indeed. He was very polite, whereas before I asked him that, he was warm. He said the church would not condone the taking of life for any reason.'

'What about all the holy wars that have taken place in the name of one god or another?'

'I didn't even go there. I may want to talk to him again, so I didn't want to totally alienate him.'

Cassie giggled and held up her glass again. 'Here's to conspiracy theorists.'

'Hear, hear,' replied Wen.

CHAPTER EIGHTEEN

Cassie woke the following morning to bright sunshine piercing the partly open blinds and a hangover from hell.

She was just trying to work out where she was and why, when a tap on her door made her move her head more quickly than was good for her. 'Ouch!'

Wen came into the room, armed with a tray. 'Morning. I've brought you coffee, toast, and more importantly, two paracetamols.'

Cassie sat up gingerly.' Thank you,' she said, as the tray was placed on her knee.

'There are towels in the bathroom, and I've found some clothes that should fit you.'

Memories flooded back. 'Was there a second bottle of wine?' Cassie asked, one eye shut against the light.

'There was.' Wen smiled.

'And did I drink most of it?'

'About ninety-eight per cent. Now, drink your coffee, take the painkillers, and try to eat some toast.'

'I need to phone the hospital.'

'Done. They're both doing well. See you downstairs in about half an hour? 'And with that, Wen left Cassie to it.

Not long after Wen's breakfast delivery, there was a knock on the front door.

Now, Rose stood in Wen's hallway, having just arrived for her first day as Daisy's nanny. Aran was taking her through his house rules.

'Let Rose take off her coat and sit down, Aran, before you bombard her.' Wen took Rose's bag and coat. 'Come through, Rose.'

'I was just telling Rose about the layout of the house.' Aran followed them into the kitchen. 'Anyway, I have made notes for you, and I will be upstairs if you need any advice.'

Daisy was, as usual when anyone else was about, being good as gold. Right now, she was playing with her toes and blowing bubbles, showing that she could indeed multitask.

'I'll be going to Liverpool with my colleague today,' Wen said. 'I'll be back in Warrington from mid-afternoon, if all goes well. Rose, you have my number, but I'm sure Aran can answer any questions.'

Wen told Rose where all Daisy's things were, then happy that her child was in good hands, sat down and had another cup of tea while she waited for Cassie.

***

Leonard Deed paced his office. Things were crowding in on him, getting out of control. The worst of it was that he had no one he could ask for counsel. One of his two companions in this conspiracy was lying in a morgue in Cheshire, and the other was sitting before him in a state of panic, having arrived unexpectedly late last night.

'Why on earth did you run, Truman? And why here?'

'Grand Master, I escaped with minutes to spare. Those two detectives must have arrived after I drove away. I just hope they're all right.'

'There were two attackers, you say? Strangers?'

'Yes, two. Men, I think. If I hadn't been held up at the bank, I would be dead now. As I turned onto my street, I saw them going through my gate and I just kept driving. I didn't know where else to go.'

Leo stopped pacing and sat down. 'Well, you can't stay here. I will arrange a safe place for you.'

'Where? And for how long? Grand Master, this is madness. We need to destroy The Book before it falls into the wrong hands or more people die.'

'Truman, have you any idea how many lives have been lost over the centuries while protecting The Book?'

Professor Gryfinn shook his head.

'Hundreds, if not thousands. And for good reason.'

'Yes, I know. But these people will not stop. Look what they did to Michael.'

'This is our lot. We were given this sacred task and all that goes with it.' Leo sighed and rested his head on the back of his chair. 'Go and get some sleep, then Mark will take you to one of our houses. You can stay there for the next few days while we put a plan together.'

'Yes, Grand Master, and thank you.'

'Don't thank me yet, Truman. We have a very delicate situation here that needs a long-term solution.'

***

'I've got Wild's blessing for us to interview Susan from the café and Jessica Tong,' Wen told Cassie, as they drove towards Liverpool. 'He's up to his eyes looking for whoever attacked Colin and Ruby.'

Cassie was sipping strong coffee from a travel mug. Her brain seemed to be lagging.

'The Liverpool team have spoken to them already, but the witnesses know we want to question them as well. How do you feel?'

'All right. Well, better than I did at eight this morning. I'm sorry I got so drunk.'

'Cassie, we've all been there. You had a shit day. I'm just glad you came to me and didn't spend the evening alone.' She paused. 'I take it there's no one special in your life at the moment?'

'I'm not very good at relationships Wen. Every time I meet someone, I go at it too hard and frighten them off.'

'What, you ask them if they want kids on your first date? That sort of thing?'

Cassie laughed.' Not quite that bad, but you're not far off.'

Wen glanced at her friend.' You'll meet someone one day, trust me.'

'Can we go to the hospital afterwards and see Colin and Ruby?'

'That's the plan,' said Wen as she indicated to come off the motorway.

'I don't know what else I can tell you.' Susan Hampshore had taken the two detectives into the back of the café while another colleague carried on serving. 'This must be my fourth interview with the police.' She seemed irritated at the level of interrogation she was undergoing. And honestly, Cassie couldn't blame her.

'I'm sorry, Susan,' she replied.' You've been so patient. However, there have been further developments, so we just wanted to go over your statement again.'

'What sort of developments?'

'I can't go into detail, but two police officers were seriously injured in Liverpool yesterday when they were following up a lead on this case.' Cassie tried to sip her coffee but the travel mug was empty.

Susan took the mug from Cassie.' Let me fill that for you. Coffee?'

'Thank you. Yes, coffee. Black, please.'

'And you, Detective Chief Inspector?'

'Could I just have a glass of water please, Susan,' said Wen, sitting back. She had allowed Cassie to lead on the interview, as she was a familiar face to Susan.

Drinks provided; the three women sat around a worktop. A large oven beside them threw out heat and a delicious smell of baking.

'So, what do you want to know?' asked Susan.

'When the professor and the priest were sitting together, did you notice anything being passed between them?' Cassie asked as she opened her notebook.

'No. That's what the other two asked. What I mean is, I was serving customers, so I wasn't watching them particularly. It's always busy here.'

'They didn't touch each other, or anything on the table?'

'No. Except…'

'Except?' Wen put her head on one side.

'The professor left his newspaper on the table when he got up to leave. He always did the *Times* crossword over his coffee break. I used to say to him, "Can't you give that brain of yours a rest, Prof?"' Susan looked down, her mouth trembling.

'So usually he took his paper with him?' said Cassie.

'Yes, always. Anyway, when I went to clear their table, it wasn't there. I remember because I was going to rescue it and give it back to him the next time I saw him. But I didn't, did I? See him again, I mean.' She was now crying quietly.

'Could someone else have picked up the paper?' Wen asked gently. 'Another customer, maybe?'

Susan shook her head. 'No. I went to clear the table as soon as they both left.'

Cassie and Wen exchanged a glance. 'Thank you, Susan, you've been very helpful. And I'm sorry that this has upset you,' said Cassie.

'Yes, the other professor called in to see Professor Johan,' Jessica Tong said, in a matter-of-fact way.

Cassie rolled her eyes. 'And why didn't you mention this when we saw you before?'

'You didn't ask?' Jessica shot back.

'But it might be important, Jessica,' Cassie said, exasperated.

Jessica shrugged. 'I was stressed, and when I'm stressed I go to pieces. I didn't think it mattered. Visitors with passes go in and out of the offices all the time. Professor Gryfinn was a good friend and colleague of Professor Johan. He often popped in.'

'The day he called, was he looking for anything?' asked Wen.

'No, I don't think so. But I had to leave the office for ten minutes, so I wasn't there the whole time.'

'Did he say why he was calling?' asked Cassie.

'No, just that he was here to see his friend. I thought perhaps they had made arrangements for lunch, or they were going to do some more work on that book.'

'They worked on it a lot, did they?' asked Wen.

'Well, they did when you first found it. Just on the photos that he'd taken, of course. Are you the police officers who found it?'

'Yes,' said Wen. 'Professor Johan told Gryfinn we had a copy, did he?'

'Oh yes. They were both here waiting for it to arrive that day. In fact, Professor Johan got really worked up when it was late. He kept saying that even if you were driving the long way round, you should have been here.'

Cassie looked at Wen. 'Johan knew your route?'

'Yes. He wanted to know what time we would arrive, down to the minute. I told him we were planning on taking the A57 rather than the motorway.'

'So if he knew—'

'So did Gryfinn!'

As they drove to the hospital to visit their colleagues, the two women had a lot to think about.

Jessica had helped more than she knew, but they still didn't know if Professor Gryfinn had looked for, or indeed found anything when he visited his friend's office that day. But the discovery that he might have had something to do with the ambush of Wen and Jeff – that was a step forward.

In addition, the priest might have handed something to Professor Johan. Or had it been the other way round? Could the professor have hidden something inside his newspaper for Father Michael to see?

When they arrived at the hospital, further good news awaited them. Colin had come round and was making sense. In fact, the medical staff were having difficulty in stopping him from discharging himself. He was now in a normal hospital room away from ICU, which was reassuring.

He smiled as Cassie walked in, followed by Wen. 'Boss. And DCI. You didn't both need to visit.' His head was swathed in bandages and his eyes were swollen, but he was bright, which was a great relief to both his bosses.

'Now then, Colin,' said Cassie, 'what's all this nonsense about discharging yourself?'

He looked at Cassie, shamefaced.' I changed my mind when I tried to get up and the room started spinning. How's Ruby? They said she's having an op tomorrow.'

'We came here first. I'll pop back after I've seen Ruby and let you know how she's getting on,' said Cassie. 'Can you remember what happened?'

'We went to Professor Gryfinn's front door and got no answer. I went round the back of the house. I heard a noise behind me and then' – he pointed to his head – 'this happened.'

Wen sat on the end of Colin's bed. 'You didn't see anyone?'

'I did, actually, out of the corner of my eye. At least, I think I did. But whoever hit me did it from behind.'

'Two people, then. Have Wild's lot been in to talk to you?' Cassie enquired.

'First thing. I hadn't even had my breakfast.' Colin said this with a smile. 'They reckon we stopped whoever it was from breaking in. Said something about burglary.'

'Yes, well, we don't think that holds water,' Cassie said firmly. 'Did you know Gryfinn has disappeared?'

'Yes. That stinks of involvement, doesn't it?' Colin winced.

'Are you in pain?' Wen looked about for a nurse.

'It's OK. I just get the odd shooting pain where they drilled into my skull.'

Now Cassie winced. 'We'll go and look in on Ruby. Stay put, Colin, and do as the staff tell you.'

'That's what I've been saying.' A middle-aged woman stood in the doorway, a drink in one hand and a pack of sandwiches in the other. She was about five foot five, with a sandy bob and glasses, and you didn't have to be a detective to realise that she was a relative of Colin's.

'This is my mum,' he said. 'Mum, these two ladies are my bosses.'

Cassie held out her hand.' Hello, Mrs Briggs. I'm DI Rowden. We spoke yesterday.'

Colin's mother shook her hand warmly. 'Thank you so much for arranging a car to bring me here. Colin's father is away with the army, and I don't like driving in the city.'

'No problem at all.' Colin came from a quiet town in Cumbria called Dalton-in-Furness, so the Cumbria police had taken her part-way, then handed her over to Cheshire Police at a motorway service station.

'He's doing well,' Colin's mother told them. 'But he's coming home with me as soon as he's well enough to be discharged. I'll get him properly better.'

'Mum, there's no need.'

Cassie and Wen could hear the conversation continuing as they went in search of Ruby's ward.

Ruby looked much worse than Colin. Her face was still very swollen and all shades of blue and purple. She tried to smile, but it was so fleeting that it barely counted.

'Hi there, Ruby, how are you today?' asked Cassie.

Ruby pointed her thumb down and mouthed 'pain.'

'Colin was asking after you,' said Wen. 'He's doing OK. 'Ruby managed a slight nod.

A woman, presumably Ruby's mother, appeared. 'She's off to theatre when the swelling goes down.' She didn't sound as relaxed as Mrs Briggs.

The two women introduced themselves. 'Will she get compensation for this?' Ruby's mother asked briskly.

'That's certainly a possibility,' Wen said slowly. She could see Ruby's discomfort at her mother's question, even through her injuries.

'Good. Because she'll need something to live off while she recovers and looks for a new career.'

Ruby was shaking her head. 'We can support Ruby through this, Mrs Wall,' said Wen. 'And Ruby should only make decisions about her career when she's fully recovered.'

'I don't know what she was thinking. The police, for God's sake!'

'Ruby is very good at her job,' said Cassie. 'She could go far in the police force.'

'Or get herself killed. Look at her! I didn't even recognise my own daughter when I came in.' Ruby's mother sniffled, then burst into tears.

Wen helped her to a seat. 'This has been a terrible shock for you, Mrs Wall, but I've seen so many people with injuries like this. It looks much worse than it is. Ruby will be just fine.' Wen spoke with conviction, and hoped she was right.

CHAPTER NINETEEN

'You're saying that Professor Gryfinn is somehow connected with Dr Morgan's death?' Wild rubbed the back of his neck.

'It's a possibility,' Wen replied, though she had no doubt that he was. She also had no proof. Just the words of Jessica Tong, who had already shown herself an inconsistent witness, with her ideas of what was important and what was not.

Wild looked unsettled. 'I'd like to talk to him.'

'Wouldn't we all,' said Cassie.

Wild frowned. 'I'll ignore that, Detective Inspector Rowden, as you have had two officers seriously assaulted.'

Cassie opened her mouth to reply but Wen got in first. 'Any sightings of Gryfinn?'

'No. We've put out an APB, but he's vanished. He could be anywhere.'

'Any further leads on your burglars?' Wen gave Cassie a warning look as she asked this.

DCI Wild huffed. 'I suppose I do have to apologies there. Our original suspects have an alibi, so maybe the perpetrators were at Gryfinn's house to harm him for some reason. Let's face it, we have seen some very violent crimes recently. He's obviously involved in this investigation, to a greater or lesser degree.'

'And my officers got beaten up inst—'

'Right, DCI Wild, we'll head back to Warrington,' said Wen. 'Keep us informed of any further developments, please, and we'll be in touch soon.' She took Cassie firmly by the arm and steered her towards the door. 'Come on, Cassie, hold it together,' she murmured as they made for the exit.

It wasn't until they were back on the M62 that Cassie found her voice. 'That man!'

'What about that man?'

'He's mishandled the case from the get-go. I should have been more assertive when we were questioning those witnesses the first time round.'

'Maybe. But it's difficult when you're on someone else's patch. Let's get back to base and go over all this information again with the team.'

'What's left of it,' said Cassie. 'You, me, and Jake.'

'Yes, we are a bit thin on the ground. Think anyone from the wider team is up to joining us?'

'There's Daisy Pinkman and Peter Blake. What do you think?'

'Daisy I know, and I agree she's up to it,' said Wen. 'Peter's new to me.'

Cassie considered. 'He's a bit cocky, but under that I think he's quite unsure of himself. He's got a degree in criminal psychology. Peter's actually very clever, but he puts on an act to prove he's one of the boys.'

'Do you think he'd work well with Daisy?'

Cassie smiled. 'Daisy will soon form him into someone she likes.'

***

Leo put down the phone, feeling as if the weight of the world was on his shoulders. He closed his eyes and tried to control his breathing.

Bright sunshine flooded into his study. It was another beautiful summer's day. Such a pity that his mood didn't reflect the warmth and light trying to invade his surroundings.

A tap at his door brought him back to the everyday. 'Come.'

Mark opened the door and entered. 'You wished to see me, Grand Master?'

Mark Spencer was tall and thin, with a neat beard. He always wore a dark suit, white shirt and black tie. Leo had inherited Mark from his predecessor, and though their relationship could never have been described as close, each knew with certainty that they could depend on the other.

'Yes. Have we managed to find a suitable place for our friend to stay? For now, at any rate?'

'Yes, Grand Master. I thought the flat at Golders Green.'

'Ah, yes. Perfect. The Professor will blend in there nicely. Take him there later today, will you?'

'Yes, Grand Master.' Mark turned to go.

'Oh, and Mark…'

'Yes, Grand Master?'

'We must find a more permanent solution to the problem.'

'I'll give that some thought, Grand Master,' said Mark, and left the room.

***

Daisy was tall and blonde and wore black jacket and trousers with a white T-shirt underneath. She was thirty-four, divorced with no children, and reliable and thorough. Peter was lanky, and looked as if he needed to grow into his clothes. Blake grinned from ear to ear. 'You want us on the team?'

'Try not to look so pleased, DC Blake,' said Cassie. ' This is only because two colleagues have been badly hurt.'

'Yes, of course. Sorry, boss.'

Daisy Pinkman smiled. 'Thank you for your confidence, boss.'

They were in the DI's office with Cassie and Wen, to be brought up to date. Jake was supposed to be there too, but so far, he was a no-show.

Cassie looked at her watch again and let out a deep sigh. 'We'd better make a start. Does anyone know where Jake is?'

'No, boss,' said Peter. 'He just said he had to pop out and he wouldn't be long.'

'Right. I'll bring him up to date—'

Jake threw the door open, out of breath. 'Sorry, boss.' He nodded at Wen. ' Boss.'

'Jake, where the hell have you been? 'Cassie said.

'To see Ruby. 'Jake sat down in the now-crowded office.

'Ruby?'

'Yes, Ruby. 'Jake sounded defensive.

'Oh. I see.' Cassie decided she would speak to Jake later, but what could she say? She couldn't tell him he had no right to visit his friend and colleague in hospital. And she knew he would be more than happy to make up the time. They often had to tell him to go home when they were working on something big.

'How is she?' asked Daisy.

'A mess. Her face… 'He bowed his head for a moment, then looked up. 'Right. What's new? We need to get these bastards.'

Cassie and Wen went through everything from start to finish to enable the two new officers to get up to speed, since they had only heard snippets during general briefings.

Jake took copious notes, stating he wanted to be sure he hadn't missed anything, while Daisy and Peter listened intently, jotting down the odd bullet point here and there.

'That's where we find ourselves.' Cassie leaned back in her chair. She felt shattered, both physically and mentally. She knew some of that was down to her over-indulgence the night before, but mostly it was not being able to get a grip on this case.

'Any ideas?' Wen asked the team.

'Still no trace of Professor Gryfinn?' asked Jake.

'No.' Cassie threw her pen on the desk. 'A motorway camera captured his car heading south yesterday after the attack, but nothing since.'

'Heading to London, then?'

Cassie sighed. 'Possibly, Jake, but he could have been heading to a port, an airport, St Pancras… I don't think we'll see him again.'

'I'll do a search on him,' said Jake. 'See where he goes when he's not in Liverpool. Where he takes holidays, who his friends are.'

Wen shrugged. 'Liverpool murder team say he has no relatives in this country and seldom goes anywhere.'

'I'm not having that,' Jake responded. 'He does things and goes places: he just doesn't want anyone to know about it. But unless he pays cash for everything, I'll find him.'

***

Inspector Luca Vella was also enjoying a beautiful summer

day in Malta. As he sat in his office in Valletta, trying to make the most of the light breeze that made the heat just bearable, he was reading the report which had been put on his desk earlier that day.

He read it through once, then a second time. 'Alessia,' he shouted, to his female colleague next door. '*Alessia!*'

She came through the open door which separated their rooms. 'Yes, what? You don't need to shout.'

'Have you seen this?' He got up and handed her the document he had been engrossed in moments before.

'No, what is it?' Alessia started to skim the first page. As she read further, her eyes widened. 'Is this real?'

'As far as we know. But let's be honest, what has been real about this case? I need to contact the teams in England straight away. In the meantime, can you find out why we are only just seeing this now?'

CHAPTER TWENTY

It was luck that Wen was still in the office when Luca messaged Cassie to arrange a Zoom meeting. Minutes later, he was on screen. 'Sorry to disturb you, Detectives, but I thought this was too important to leave.'

'Not at all, Luca,' said Cassie, with a smile.' Seeing you unexpectedly is the highlight of what has otherwise been a shit couple of days.' She explained what had happened over the past forty-eight hours.

'Good God! And how are your officers?'

'Doing all right so far, thank you. But somebody really doesn't want the artefact to fall into the wrong hands. We have a suspect at last, even if he has disappeared for now.'

'And I may have another lead.' Luca said this with a satisfied grin. 'I tried to get DCI Wild on the call too, but he's away from his desk. I left him a message to contact me ASAP.'

Wen moved her chair closer to the laptop screen.

'Let me take you back to the day when your Professor Johan was murdered and our Dr Dolenz met his untimely death,' began Luca. 'If you recall, we managed to find Dr Dolenz's laptop.'

'Yes,' said Wen. 'He gave it to his neighbour for safekeeping, didn't he?'

'Exactly. But when we managed to unlock it, which was no mean feat, I can tell you, there was very little of interest. That made us wonder why he had gone to the trouble of hiding it in the first place.'

'And why he put his neighbour in potential danger, because he obviously thought there was a real threat to his life,' Cassie added.

'That's what we thought. So I let our IT geeks keep the laptop. They started searching for deleted files, and two days ago they found this.' Luca shared a document to the screen. Both women leaned in to peer at it.

'OK,' said Cassie, 'what is it? That's not any language I know.'

'It's Latin. Dr Dolenz taught Latin at the University of Malta one day a week after he retired. He would have been the guy we went to to get this translated. Only he's—'

'Dead,' finished Wen.

'Which is why we've only just received this. We had to find another translator, and hey presto.' The document changed into another foreign language, presumably Maltese.

'Still no help, Luca.' Cassie tapped her pen on the desk.

A dark-haired woman appeared beside Luca. 'He's showboating. He loves an audience, especially when they are beautiful women.'

'This is my partner, Alessia Borg,' said Luca. 'Work partner, you understand. I'm not her type, sadly.'

Cassie couldn't hold back a smile.

'Get on with it, Luca, or you will lose your audience,' said Alessia.

'She's so bossy.' Luca pushed his partner away gently. 'I will give you the highlights. Even as I speak, this is being translated into English, and we will send you the translation in about an hour.'

Both Cassie and Wen took out their notebooks.

'Basically,' began Luca, 'Dolenz had a lead on the original artefact. He thought it was in Cyprus, where the Knights Templar lived for a short while after they ran from persecution. Indeed, that is where he and the professor intended to go after meeting up in Malta.'

'What changed?' asked Wen.

'The doctor sensed he was being followed. And just before he was murdered, he returned from the university to find his house had been searched. He always took his laptop with him to work, so they didn't find what they were looking for.'

'This doesn't really change things though, Luca, does it?' Cassie's anticipation of another lead was now starting to dissipate, leaving her feeling very flat.

'It's what he wrote towards the end of this document that's interesting. He fears the Priory, and we know this name. They are a small group of zealots who answer to no one. They feel it is their duty to guard holy relics, and they will go to any lengths to do this. They use hired assassins on occasion and are led by one man, known as the Teacher of the Temple.'

'The Teacher of the Temple could mean anything or anyone,' Cassie said to Wen, after the call had ended.

'I'm off, Cassie,' Wen replied. 'I need to mull this over. I'll be in tomorrow, probably about nine, and we can put our heads together then. I think we both need a good night's sleep.' She patted Cassie on the arm and left the office.

Cassie put her head in her hands. Wen was right: she needed to go home for a bath and an early night. Maybe things would seem clearer in the morning. But somehow, she doubted it.

***

Wen arrived home to peace and tranquillity. Daisy was lying on a rug in the open lounge area by the kitchen. Rose was sitting on the floor beside her, talking as she tidied Daisy's toys, such as they were for one so young.

'You two look as if you're friends already,' said Wen, as she put her bag on the table.

Rose put her hand to her chest. 'Oh, you made me jump.'

'Sorry to startle you. How has she been?'

'Very good, apart from some colic after her lunchtime bottle. She was Miss Grumpy for a while then. But we went for a nice long walk in the sun and she got off to sleep.'

Wen was relieved. 'I thought it was me. She never seems to get colic when she's with Aran.'

Rose shook her head. 'It's just a phase. I know it's easy for me to say that, but it will pass.' It felt strange taking advice from a teenager, even if she was due to turn twenty in a matter of weeks. 'I asked Aran if he wanted to come with us. He was trying to soothe her while I got the pram ready.'

'But he said no?'

Rose nodded. 'He said he never goes out.'

'True. Well, hardly ever. I could get him out now and again until a madman threatened to kill him. Since then, it has just got worse.'

Rose looked shocked. 'That's terrible.'

'Yes, it was a bad time for him. My partner was helping him with therapy, but...' Wen trailed off, not wanting to go down that particular rabbit hole just yet with her nanny.

'How did he manage when you were in hospital? That must have been so stressful for him.'

'He was in a shocking state. My officers tried to persuade him to go to the hospital with them, but he just couldn't. It was Mrs Guess, our cleaner, who brought him to visit me in the end.'

'Yes, I met her today. She's lovely, isn't she?'

'Yes, she is.' *Maybe it's just me she doesn't like,* mused Wen. 'She's the only other person Aran is completely comfortable with. She took him to the hospital and stayed with him the first time. After that, she picked him up each day and dropped him off at the hospital, and he would call her when he needed to come home. I owe her a lot. We both do.'

'I've not seen much of him today.'

'That's normal, Rose. I don't see much of him, and I live here.'

'He did leave me some salad for my lunch, though. It was in the fridge when I got back from our walk, with a post-it on the fridge door saying it was for me.'

That's surprising, thought Wen, but she kept that to herself.

***

Cassie almost fell asleep in the bath, which hardly ever happened, and the water was tepid by the time she got out.

Now she was in bed watching TV. She had set it to switch off in an hour, almost sure she would be well asleep before that.

She was being chased by a hooded man with a burning cross. He was calling her name and laughing. And then she was in the bell tower of a church, and the bells were ringing so loud that she had to cover her ears.

Cassie awoke with a gasp, drenched in sweat, her heart thumping against her ribcage. Her phone was ringing. She glanced at the clock as she made a grab for her mobile, wincing at the noise. It was four in the morning.

'Hello,' she muttered.

'Is that Detective Inspector Rowden?' said a cheery male voice. Instantly, Cassie wanted to slap him.

'Yes, that's me.' She blinked herself more awake.

'Sorry to bother you, ma'am. It's DC Phillips here, Metropolitan Police. A gentleman with serious injuries has been admitted to the Royal Free Hospital, and he's asking for you.'

Cassie was now wide awake. 'Me? Are you sure?'

'Yes, ma'am. He had your card in his wallet. He said it's imperative that he speaks to you. That he hasn't got long. I must say, he isn't making much sense, because the medics here say he should recover. Anyhow, he insisted I phone you straight away. Sorry for the early call.'

'Has this man got a name? I presume that if he has a wallet there's some form of ID.'

'Yes, ma'am. His name is Truman Gryfinn.'

CHAPTER TWENTY-ONE

'What time is your train?' Wen had also been in a deep sleep when her phone woke her at four thirty.

'It's five fifty-seven from Bank Quay. Gets into Euston at eight. The Met are sending someone to meet me.' As Cassie talked, she was putting her laptop, charger and a file into a messenger bag.

'Are you sure you don't want me to come?'

'No, honestly, I'll be back this afternoon. What would be great is if you could go into the office, speak to DCI Wild, and generally do what you do.'

'All right. I was going to come in today anyway. What do you want me to tell the DCI about Gryffin?'

'Just say he's turned up in London and the Met want me to talk to him. Make it up as you go along, Wen. I just don't want him to know that Gryfinn is injured in hospital and asked for me. Be vague.'

Wen laughed. 'With my sleep deprivation, that's not uncommon. Keep in touch.'

Of course, the train was late. Only by ten minutes, but Cassie liked to get to places ahead of time, so she had been on a chilly platform for almost half an hour by the time the train pulled in. For some reason, only the waiting room on the opposite side of the platform was open.

Cassie was amazed at just how many people were getting on the train, and upgraded to Premium Plus as soon as she boarded. At least she could work in comfort and grab a roll and a coffee for breakfast as soon as they got going.

She had told DC Phillips which train she would be on, and though he would then be off duty, he had arranged for someone else to meet her at Euston.

She had also asked him to email her a short report of what had happened so far with Gryfinn. Now she was reading through it, trying to get straight in her head what was waiting for her at the end of the line.

According to hospital staff, the injured man had been brought into A&E by ambulance at five past three in the morning, having been found on the A502 in Golders Green. On admission he had been very confused, but there were no signs of a head injury. On examination, however, he had lacerations to his torso and bruised ribs. One rib was fractured, which had caused a haemothorax: his lung had bled and collapsed. The medical staff had inserted a chest drain for this, with good effect. Gryffin also had cuts on his arms, suggesting he had tried to defend himself from being stabbed. A toxicology report showed a large amount of heroin in his bloodstream. When the police had tried to interview him, he had begun talking about plots and murders. That was when the Met's CID had been called in.

'What have you been up to, Professor?' murmured Cassie.

***

Wen got to the squad room at eight thirty. 'Briefing in ten minutes, people,' she called. 'If you want to grab a coffee and something to eat, now's the time to do it.' She walked through to the office, sat down in her old seat and smiled. It felt good to be back in her rightful place.

She dialled Brendan Wild's number and he answered quickly. 'DCI Wild.'

'Hello, Brendan, Wen Price here. Just wanted to bring you up to speed on the investigation.'

'Oh, yes. Good morning, Wen. All up to speed, thank you: spoke to young Luca yesterday evening. I must say, he's a bit out there with all this stuff about secret societies and plots. I think he reads too many thrillers.' He chuckled.

'That's good. But we've had more intel since then. In the early hours, in fact.'

'And what might that be?' His voice had changed: now he sounded uncertain, almost threatened.

'Professor Gryfinn has been located in London. In fact, he's been detained.' She didn't add that he was being detained in a hospital bed, too badly injured to run anywhere.

'I'll get some of my officers on to it straight away Wen. Where is he being held?'

'Don't worry, Brendan, it's all under control. DI Rowden will be there by now. I'll get back to you later and let you know how it went.'

'Excuse me, this is *my* investigation! Who do you think you are?'

'I think you mean *our* investigation, Brendan. And I know exactly who I am. I'll speak to you later.' With that, she hung up. There would be some sort of backlash, of course. Brendan Wild wasn't the sort of man who would take well to being superseded by anyone, but especially not by a woman.

***

Cassie reached her destination at around the time that Wen was speaking to Wild. The train had been twenty minutes late arriving at Euston, and morning rush hour had delayed her arrival at the Royal Free Hospital.

Finally, she was sitting beside Truman Gryfinn. He was asleep, hooked up to monitors, drips and tubes of all descriptions. Her skin prickled. She hated hospitals, and her stay in intensive care last year hadn't helped.

Cassie was relieved to see a police officer on guard outside the room. She feared the person who had attacked Gryffin might come back for a second try.

The patient stirred. He groaned and turned his head, aware that he was not alone. The fear in his eyes was pathetic, but it disappeared when he realised who was sitting next to him. 'You came.' His voice was weak, but his relief was palpable.

'Professor, who did this to you?' Cassie kept her voice low. She wasn't sure if that was because of the patient's situation, or because she was afraid someone might hear.

'That doesn't matter.' Gryfinn took a laboured breath. 'It's the Grand Master.'

'What? The Grand Master of the Temple Church?' Cassie wasn't sure what he meant. She wasn't sure that he knew, either.

'He knows.' His eyes closed and he slipped out of consciousness. Cassie wanted to shake him awake, but thought that might be frowned upon by the medical staff. Instead, she sat beside him patiently, and emailed Wen to let her know that she was at the hospital.

A nurse popped her head into the room. 'We need to sort this man out,' she said quietly, with a friendly smile. 'Why don't you go and get yourself a coffee.'

'I'll wait outside.' There was no way Cassie would leave her witness until he had said more.

She got up. Gryfinn's eyes flew open and he grabbed her hand. 'Don't leave me,' he begged. 'They will kill me.'

Cassie gently unpeeled his fingers from her arm. 'No one is going to kill you. Not on my watch.' She gave him what she hoped was a reassuring smile.

'No. They will kill me. I know too much. I need to talk to you, now.'

Cassie looked at the nurse. 'Can you give us a minute, please? This is important.'

The nurse opened her mouth to say something.

'Please,' Cassie said again.

The nurse nodded and disappeared.

Cassie sat back down. 'Right, Truman, it's just me and you. What do you need to tell me?'

***

Wen had given the whole team a rundown of the inquiry so far, then invited the smaller team into the office. As they collected their notes, remarks such as 'teacher's pet' were made, with somewhat rude replies.

Wen was checking her emails as they filed in. She was relieved to see that Cassie had arrived at her destination safely. She didn't know why, but she felt she should have gone with her. 'Right, team. What have you got for me?'

'I've done a search for Gryfinn's financials,' said Jake. 'He's not short of a bob or two and he doesn't use his cards much, which doesn't help me. On the day he fled, he took a sizeable amount of cash from the bank and filled up with petrol at a services south of Watford Gap. But as we know he's in London, that doesn't help much. His two previous big spends were buying plane tickets to Rome and booking accommodation there.'

'I followed up with a phone call to the hotel he used last time,' said Daisy. 'They said he often came on short breaks. They thought he was doing research for the church.'

'I'm amazed you found someone who spoke English so quickly,' remarked Wen.

'She speaks fluent Italian, boss,' said Peter.

'Do you now? Any other languages?'

'French and Spanish. I have an ear for languages.' Daisy had gone slightly pink.

'Going back to the hotel, Daisy, did they say why they thought he was doing research for the church?'

'He met up with a priest on each visit. It's hard to be sure, but the description they gave sounded like Father Michael.'

Wen made some notes. 'So they knew each other, at the very least.'

Jake coughed. 'I also tried to establish where Gryfinn was on the night when Father Michael was killed, and the morning when Johan was stabbed. He had bought tickets for a concert on the night the priest was murdered.'

'But that doesn't mean he went to it,' said Peter, making a note.

'True,' Jake replied. 'He doesn't have any alibi for the morning of Professor Johan's attack.'

'Do we think he actually did the deed?' said Wen. 'My feeling is that he was involved, but in whatever murky group he belongs to, he was at a level where he wouldn't get his hands dirty.'

Everyone nodded and Jake leaned forward. 'The DI might be able to shed more light on his involvement once she has interviewed him.'

'I wonder why he asked for her in particular?' said Daisy.

'Not sure,' said Wen. 'DI Rowden can't remember giving Gryffin one of her business cards. She gave one to Professor Johan when he visited the station last year, though.' She couldn't see why Gryfinn would have got a card from his friend. But if he was involved with the murders, was Johan really his friend?

***

'I didn't know they were going to kill that man.' Gryfinn was trying to put things in the right order. 'I knew they wanted the copy of The Book, but I never thought in my wildest dreams that they would kill.'

'Who are *they*, Professor?'

'The Priory.' He groaned and contorted with pain. This was obviously hard for him, physically and mentally. 'And then they killed Johan and Dolenz, and that beautiful priest…'

'But do we have some names? Even one name?' Truman seemed to be rambling now, and Cassie despaired of getting any more sense out of him.

'That was the last straw, for me. When they killed Michael in such a hideous way.' He started crying. 'We were very close. It's such a waste.'

Cassie attempted a new approach. 'Why did they kill those men, Professor?'

'They destroyed the copy as soon as they got it. But then Dolenz found a clue to the whereabouts of the original and it all started again. It was a lie of course. Johan and Dolenz had been drip-fed lies. I told the Grand Master I couldn't do it any more. All this killing.'

'What is so important about this book that people will kill for it?'

'It's the word of Jesus. But not the words people want to hear. It's not… 'He beckoned her. 'Come closer.'

Cassie leaned towards him.

'Don't trust Spencer,' he whispered.

'Who's Spencer?'

'I need to tell you, but I can't.'

'Yes, you can. You can trust me, Professor.'

'If I tell you, they will kill you too. I've already put you in danger. Get to the Grand Master today, or it might be too late.' He began coughing violently, and then there was blood. Lots of blood.

'Nurse!' Cassie screamed, and pushed the emergency bell. Within seconds the room was full of people giving orders, asking for drugs, demanding to know oxygen levels.

Cassie got squeezed to the back of the room and out through the door, but she had no doubt in her mind that the professor was already dead.

CHAPTER TWENTY TWO

'What do you think you're doing, DCI Price? Shutting out our Liverpool colleagues, almost to the point of being rude?' Chief Superintendent Charles Manning had turned an unpleasant shade of red, and Wen feared for his blood pressure.

'I'm sorry, sir, if it came across like that. No disrespect was meant. We had it in hand, that was all. I couldn't have notified the DCI sooner: DI Rowden was on the train when she emailed me.' Wen had her fingers crossed behind her back. 'She knows how little sleep I've been getting with the baby, and didn't want to wake me. By the time I got that email, she would have been halfway to London.'

'Oh. All right.' The bluster had gone. 'I know Brendan Wild from the Free— from some charity work we do together. I'll give him a call and try to pour oil on troubled waters. I know he can be a bit over the top sometimes.

'Thank you so much, sir. I appreciate that. He has seemed rather stressed. But then, I don't know him as you do.'

'Yes. Well. This case is important to him. He's up for promotion, and you are only as good as the outcome of your last case.' Manning picked up the phone. 'Keep him updated, DCI Price.'

Wen took that as her dismissal. 'I will, sir,' she said sweetly as she closed the door behind her.

Back in the squad room, Wen decided to email Cassie. Firstly, she was desperate to know what had happened at the hospital. Secondly, she wanted to tell Cassie the reason for Wild's less than co-operative work ethic: he wanted all the credit because he was up for promotion. Not a good reason to be less than open with the Cheshire Serious Crime Squad, but she knew of people who would climb over their own mothers to get on.

When she looked at her emails, one had arrived from Cassie.

'Gryfinn has just died. On my way to see the Grand Master at the Temple Church. Not sure I will get back tonight after all.'

***

The taxi seemed to be taking for ever. Cassie was having palpitations, wondering how much this would cost, but the Met had said it might be half an hour or more before they could get transport to her. 'Some protest somewhere kicked off big-style,' the police officer at Gryfinn's door had informed her.

'Will you stay here, please?' Cassie asked, as she took her leave. 'I know he's dead, but this could be a crime scene.'

The constable seemed dubious. 'Do you think so?'

'I don't know, Officer. Neither do you. So please stay here until the body has been collected for a post-mortem.'

'Why is the journey taking so long?' she asked the taxi driver.

'You can't get to it by the main road, love. Got to go by back streets, like. I tell you, when I was doing the knowledge, it was places like this that got you. You know, out of the way gaffs. No sat nav for us, love.' He tapped his head. 'We carry it all up here.'

Cassie sighed. She didn't even know what she would say when she reached her destination. 'Oh, hello, Grand Master. Sorry to bother you, but are you a mass murderer? Or maybe the head of a secret society prepared to kill?' She had asked for backup, but when would it arrive?

Finally, they pulled up by the Temple Church. Cassie had emailed Jake for the Grand Master's address, and been told that his house was behind the church.

'This is as far as I can take you, love. No vehicles from this point.'

Cassie paid an eye-watering amount of money with her card, and began the short walk to the Grand Master's home.

The sun was still shining and the afternoon heat was cloying. Cassie wasn't dressed for summer. She had her usual dark suit on, and it drew the heat as a flame draws a moth.

Through some bollards, round a corner, and there it was. Cassie's first thought was *What a beautiful house.* But then she noticed something unsettling: the front door was open.

As she approached, Cassie realised she was holding her breath and told herself to relax. But no one would leave their front door open in London, surely.

She pushed the door wider and listened. Nothing. Then a noise: a cry of pain. It seemed to be coming from above. Cassie took the stairs two at a time, trying to be as quiet as possible.

'No! Please don't!' That sounded as if it came from a room down a short corridor. Cassie was rooted to the spot. What should she do? She wasn't armed. She had called for the save brigade, a joke name for a SWAT team, but what if they arrived too late?

'Ahhhhh! Please, no more!'

Cassie threw open the door of the room and saw a man on the floor, covered in blood. His torturer swung round to face Cassie.

There was a man on the floor. When he saw he shouted.' Get out of here!'

The man facing her had a lethal-looking knife in his hand and a murderous look in his eye. He was wearing a baseball cap. He looked familiar, but from where?

Cassie backed away, holding her hands up. 'Sir, please put that down. I'm a police officer and I have called for backup.' The man lunged at her. She raised her arm to protect herself and he slashed at it.

Cassie screamed at the pain and fell against the door frame. Now he was standing over her, his knife poised to strike her death blow. Cassie closed her eyes, not wanting to believe what was about to happen, and crossed herself. 'Hail Mary, full of grace—'

'That won't help you,' the man sneered.' There's got to be a God in the first place for any of that to work.'

Cassie looked into the eyes of her murderer as he raised the knife...

A shot rang out and Cassie winced. The man fell at her feet, a wound in the centre of his forehead. Then the shooter stepped over her and emptied the full magazine of their gun into the dead man.

***

Flashing lights, and people all talking at once. The man who had probably saved her life was now in handcuffs. Someone called for paramedics. Someone else wrapped a soft, fluffy white towel around Cassie's arm. Cassie thought *They'll never get these stains out* as the towel turned red, and started laughing.

Later, in the A&E department of the Royal London Hospital, Cassie briefly remembered being told that she had a very deep laceration which would have to be repaired in theatre. It was all very surreal and in the ambulance, she thought they had given her something for pain. That, with her loss of blood, had made her very fuzzy about what was going on.

***

Wen was ready to leave the police station when her office phone rang. 'Hello, DCI Price.'
'Hello, DCI Price. My name is DC Phillips. I'm with the Met.'
Wen went cold. 'How can I help you?'
'I'm calling about your DI, Cassie Rowden.'
Oh no. 'What about DI Rowden?'
'She's been involved in an incident and unfortunately she sustained an injury. Not life-threatening, so please don't be concerned. She's in hospital, being well looked after.'
'What happened?'
'She was at the home of The Grand Master of the Temple..'
'Yes. I knew she was going there, but not why.'
'I'm not sure she knew why herself, but she walked in on a crime scene, and when armed officers arrived it was a bit chaotic, to say the least.'
DC Phillips gave Wen as much information as he could, but it was very confusing. 'Four people were involved in the incident. One is dead, two are in hospital, and one is under arrest and isn't

saying much.' He sounded frustrated.

'And this all took place at the Grand Master's house?'

'Yes, ma'am.'

'Right, send me the postcode for the hospital. I'll drive down now.'

'It might be better if you waited until morning, ma'am. Your colleague will be asleep when you arrive.'

'No. I'm coming down straight away.'

Wen immediately called Rose. 'Can you stay the night? Something serious has happened and I need to go to London right now.'

'Yes, of course. What about Aran?'

She's learning fast, thought Wen. Already, Rose knew that Aran's feelings would need to be considered. 'I'll speak to Aran before I leave, Rose.'

'OK.'

'And Rose…'

'Yes?'

'Thank you.'

There was a knock at her door and Jake put his head round it. 'Boss, this came. Special delivery.' He held out a small padded envelope. It was addressed to *The officer in charge of the priest's murder*.

Wen tore it open and a pen drive fell out. There was also a note. *My brother gave this to me for safekeeping. It might help you find his murderers.*

'Damn it!' cried Wen. 'I haven't got time for this now. Cassie's been hurt and I need to get to London.'

'I'll drive you,' Jake said, at once.

'I can't ask you to do that, Jake.'

'You're not asking, I'm offering. It's not often that the grunt machine gets a proper outing.'

Wen laughed.' The grunt machine?'

'My BMW 5 series. TwinPower. Turbo. 6 cylinders. 0-62 in seven point five seconds, top speed 142 mph, but I reckon I could get 150 out of it if I really push—'

'OK, you don't need to go on. Are you sure?'

'It would be my pleasure. And if you bring your laptop, you can see what's on that.' He nodded at the pen drive. 'I'll log off.'

'I'll call Aran.'

***

Cassie woke up feeling as if someone was pushing her deep into a bed of feathers. She tried very hard to open her eyes, but they wouldn't co-operate.

'Back with us, DI Rowden,' said a man's voice at her side.

She forced her eyes open and managed to focus on the person speaking. 'Who are you?' she croaked.

'DC Will Phillips. We spoke early this morning.'

'How long have I been asleep?'

'You've been back from theatre for two hours. It's seven pm. I've notified your boss – in fact, she's on her way.'

'Why? I'll still be here tomorrow.' She frowned. 'I'm not dying, am I?'

Will laughed.' No, you're not dying.'

'What happened? At the house, I mean.' Cassie tried to sit up but that made her head spin.

'I wish I knew. The man who was shot dead was Brian Fletcher, Assistant to the Reader at the Temple Church and a barrister of some repute. The man who shot him was Mark Spencer. The Grand Master's secretary, if you can believe that.'

'The Assistant to the Reader. Of course – I've met him before.' Cassie's thoughts flicked back to when she had met Brian Fletcher. *Part of my role is education: a teacher, if you like.* That was what he had said of himself. And hadn't Luca said something about a Teacher being involved in a secret society? She couldn't think straight: she felt dizzy and nauseous.

'And that's as much as we know,' said DC Phillips. 'The Grand Master is sedated: Fletcher was torturing him. He's a mess. Severe bruising and pieces of flesh cut off him, but there's nothing that surgery and time won't heal.'

Cassie tried to concentrate. 'Gryfinn said he didn't trust

Spencer. He must have meant Mark Spencer.'

'Well, Spencer was at the Royal Free just after Gryfinn died. He must have missed you by minutes.'

'Has he said anything?' Cassie struggled to speak: her mouth was dry.

'All he's told us is that Fletcher must have followed him when he relocated Gryfinn. Apparently, Gryffin fled to the Grand Master for help. Spencer said it was most likely Fletcher who attacked the professor. He had schizophrenia, and he was in the middle of a full-blown episode.'

'Really?' Cassie found that to be a bit too convenient.

'We'll look into his medical background and see if there is any truth in that,' said Will Phillips. He shrugged, and Cassie could see doubt on his face. But she felt overwhelmed and exhausted.

'I'll leave you to rest,' said DC Phillips. 'Your DCI should be here around ten, depending on the traffic. I'll pop in again later.'

Cassie smiled as the Met officer left her. What had just happened was just unbelievable, but it had happened, and she had been in the middle of it all. She could, quite easily have died, again! This was becoming an occupational hazard she didn't even consider when she joined the force.

Even though she had felt that Wen didn't need to rush to her bedside, now she was rather glad her friend, and boss was on her way. She needed to make sense of all this, and at the moment it was too much for her to contemplate.

CHAPTER TWENTY-THREE

As they sped along in Jake's car, Wen opened her laptop and plugged in the pen drive. The drive contained a document over a hundred pages long, and she realised it must be Father Michael's manuscript.

'This will take some time.' she said to Jake.

'Well, we have a few hours. See how far you get.'

'I meant to phone the hospital for an update on Ruby and Colin today, but what with one thing and another… I seem to have too many staff as patients at the moment.'

'Well, Colin is going home to Cumbria tomorrow, and Ruby had surgery today,' said Jake.

'How is Ruby?'

'She may lose the sight in her left eye. Detached retina. They've done what they could, but the swelling disguised it.' His eyes were on the road.

'Oh, shit.' Wen's stomach twisted. She wondered what sort of impact that would have on Ruby's career, not to mention her life in general. 'Well, her mum may get her wish, then.'

Jake nodded. Presumably he knew what Wen meant.

'Right, I'll speed-read this and see if I can find anything interesting.'

The first fifty pages talked about the Knights Templar and their involvement in protecting holy relics. It told of how all the famous archaeological artefacts had disappeared, and then…

The Book of Sceleratis was discovered in a dig at Palestine in 1920 by Sir Gregory Snowhill. It was thought he was so shocked at its contents that he made a copy in code and destroyed the original. However, it is hard to believe that a man of such faith could destroy something so important.

It is now known that the original artefact was given to what remained of the Knights Templar for safekeeping, and that the last words of Jesus Christ remain hidden somewhere in England. But it is also thought that the revelations held in those words could reduce the Christian faith to ashes.

So began the struggle between the Priory and the guardian of the Book. One trying to destroy it, the other trying to preserve it but keep it hidden.

The Priory are ruthless and will let nothing stand in their way. They have killed, and will kill again, to find the book and put an end to this quest.

I know where the original is hidden, God help me. But if I am killed, no chance can be taken that I didn't give away its location, so it will be moved to another hiding place and the killings will go on.

The professor wants it to stop. I don't think I can trust him any more. The work he did on the copy revealed too much, but he couldn't be sure of what he had transcribed. With the copy missing, he and a colleague are getting close to the original – and so their lives are at risk. I must warn them.

I have seen the original, and it tested my faith to the extreme.

Jesus wrote that Pontius Pilate spared him. He replaced Our Lord with a common criminal, beaten and broken. No one would have known that it was not Jesus who was crucified that day.

In the Garden of Gethsemane, Jesus asked his father to take away this fate, and this was how the Lord God intervened.

For three days and three nights he hid in the tomb, which he then left. He did indeed have injuries from the beatings he endured before his release.

Afterwards, he visited his disciples, and together they planned how they would go out into the world and spread the word of the Lord.

Wen gasped. If this were true, there had never been a crucifixion or a resurrection. This would tip Christian belief on its head. Yet the information still gave the impression that Jesus was the son of God. What had happened to him?

'Anything interesting in there?' asked Jake.

'Oh yes', Wen replied, 'very interesting!'

***

'How are you?' The surgeon who had operated on Cassie was examining her fingers. They protruded like swollen sausages from the end of the heavy bandages which wrapped most of her right arm.

'I feel like I've been stabbed in the arm.'

The surgeon smiled. 'Is your pain manageable?'

'It's just starting to hurt again.' She winced as she moved her arm, as if she needed to prove she wasn't lying.

'I'll get the nurse to give you some IV paracetamol. I've written you up for something stronger if that doesn't do the job.' He paused. 'It was a tricky operation. The wound was very deep, and as well as severing a major blood vessel, some nerves and ligaments were damaged.'

'How bad is it?'

'Well, we've done our best, but you may require further surgery.'

'Will I have full function of my arm when I've recovered?'

He didn't meet her eyes. That, Cassie knew, was a bad sign. 'We aren't sure yet. You may have a permanent weakness in that arm.'

Cassie's brain tried to grasp what that might mean. Would she be able to drive? Work? God, would she be able to dress herself? Tears of self-pity ran down her cheeks.

The doctor patted her good arm. 'Try not to worry. There is just as much likelihood that the damage will be minimal. Pins and needles in your fingers, a slightly weaker grip.'

She nodded, and tried to pull herself together. *Hurry up and get here, Wen*, she said to herself.

***

'I need a comfort break,' said Jake, as he indicated for the services at Watford Gap.

Wen yawned. She had tried to call Cassie twice, though she would have been surprised if Cassie had answered, and left a message the second time to say they were on their way. 'I could do with a coffee,' she said, undoing her seatbelt.

The two colleagues walked towards the services building, not noticing the car which had parked just behind them. The car that had been following them ever since they left Warrington.

CHAPTER TWENTY-FOUR

A nurse woke Cassie as she checked her blood pressure. 'Sorry. It's almost impossible to do this without disturbing you.' Cassie felt the cuff around her good arm go tight. As it deflated, she let out her breath. 'That's good. I'll change this bag of fluid, and you're done for now.'

The young woman disappeared, only to return moments later with a bag of clear fluid which she swapped for the empty bag that had collapsed into itself. Once the nurse was satisfied the bag was running at the right speed, she went to the end of the bed, unhooked the chart, and wrote something. 'Can I get you anything else?' she said, looking up. 'How's the pain?'

'All right. But could I have a drink, please?'

'Of course.' The nurse helped Cassie to sit up and handed her a glass of water. 'Would you like some tea and toast?'

'Would I! Please.' It wasn't until food was mentioned that Cassie realised how hungry she was.

'Coming up.'

The nurse was on her way out when Cassie asked her the time.

'It's just after four,' she replied. 'You had a really good sleep after that paracetamol.'

Cassie glanced around her cubicle. 'Has my colleague arrived? She should be here by now. Or has she gone for a rest?'

The nurse frowned. 'Which colleague?'

'My boss. She should have been here before midnight.'

'No one has arrived to see you.'

'Are you sure?'

'Yes. I came on duty at eight last night. You've had no visitors. Oh, except that police officer.'

'Which one?'

'The one you spoke to just after you'd had your surgery.'

Cassie looked around.' Where's my bag?' She could feel her

heart speeding up.

The nurse opened Cassie's locker. 'Here it is. 'She handed it to Cassie. 'I'll sort out that tea and toast for you.'

Cassie rummaged through her bag frantically. Of course, her phone was right at the bottom. She pulled it out. No charge. 'Fuck!'

She had brought her charger, she knew she had, but she couldn't find it. In desperation, she emptied her bag onto her lap. Her charger fell out and slid onto the floor. 'Fuck! Shit!' she murmured through gritted teeth as she threw back the bedclothes and swung her legs down.

Cassie bent for the charger, and lost her balance. As she fell, something seemed to rip in her arm and a red stain crept through her bandages.

'Are you trying to lessen your chances of a full recovery, Miss Rowden?' A different doctor sat by her bed, gowned up, putting metal instruments into a tray with a clang.

The poor nurse had found Cassie on the floor, unable to get up. With assistance from other staff, she had managed to get her back to bed. Then the doctor was called to see what damage Cassie had done to herself.

It wasn't as bad as it looked, apparently. 'You've busted several sutures, but I can repair those here. No need to book a theatre slot.' And now he was almost finished.

'Last one.' He frowned as he applied the last suture. 'There. No more trying to make a run for it, do you hear me?' He snapped off his surgical gloves. 'Redress this, please, Karen.' He looked at Cassie. 'I'll see you later today.'

She apologised again, and thanked him.

Once the dressing was secured, Cassie asked the nurse, whom she now knew as Karen, whether she could pass over her phone, which had been on charge for about forty minutes.

'Here. And take it easy. I'll get you some tablets for the pain,' Karen said as she handed over the phone.

A message had been left, and when Cassie saw the time it had been sent, she felt anxious. She brought up Wen's number. It rang, and rang.

Next, she looked for DC Phillips's contact details. He answered after four rings. 'DC Phillips.'

'Will, it's Cassie Rowden. I need to see you.'

'All right, DI Rowden. I'll call on my way back when I'm off duty.'

'No. I need to see you now.'

Will Phillips rubbed the stubble on his chin. 'There's no sign of DCI Price anywhere. We're looking at the motorway CCTV, but she should have been here hours ago. Are you sure that's her car reg? She hasn't changed her car recently?'

'No, that's definitely it.'

A phone call to Aran, asking whether Wen had decided to wait until today to travel, sent him into a meltdown. 'She went with Jake! I bet he was driving too fast. I bet they had an accident. What will I do if she's had an accident?'

'Try not to worry, Aran,' said Cassie, with a lightheartedness she didn't feel. 'They probably decided to stop at a Travelodge overnight, or something.'

At least now they knew why they couldn't find Wen's car. The search began for Jake's BMW.

When Will Phillips's phone rang some forty minutes later, Cassie watched his face, trying to interpret his expression. Earlier, he had called some colleagues who worked near the services which might have been a stopping-place for Wen and Jake. 'You have? That's great news. Yes, thank you.' Will ended the call and smiled at Cassie. 'Mystery solved.'

'And?'

'They should both be here soon. Car problems.'

'What? It broke down? But why didn't Wen call?'

'The car was stolen. And they'd left everything in the car: phones, bags, coats, the lot.'

Cassie closed her eyes. 'Thank God for that.'

'They called the local police from the services and had to wait a considerable time for them to rock up. There'd been a multi-car pile-up about two miles away, so a stolen car was pretty low on their list of priorities.'

'But why didn't Wen let me know? She could have called from the services. I've been worried sick.'

'She probably thought you'd be asleep, and didn't think they'd have to wait so long for the police,' Will soothed.

Cassie drifted into a peaceful sleep once she knew that Wen and Jake were all right, and was rather put out to be woken by a gentle shake of her good arm. 'What now? My blood pressure's fine. Leave me alone,' she muttered, eyes still closed.

'Sorry,' said a familiar voice which made Cassie wake right up.

'Wen!' Cassie felt tears in her eyes and reprimanded herself for such girly behaviour.

'Hi, Cassie. Sorry we're late. We had a bit of car trouble.'

'Someone stole my baby. Bastards!' Jake was standing in the doorway looking both downcast and mutinous.

Cassie wanted to giggle, but managed to cover it with a sniff. 'Sorry, Jake. But you're both OK, that's the main thing.'

'Suppose so.' Cassie wouldn't have been surprised if he had kicked the door frame.

'Tell me what happened,' said Cassie, settling back on her pillows.

'We stopped at Watford Gap services and went for a comfort break and coffee,' said Wen. 'I just took my purse and left everything else locked in the car.'

'We were ages in the services: a coach-load had just arrived,' said Jake, with a sour look on his face. 'And when we got back to where we'd left the car, it had gone.'

'The rest I know. Well, the highlights, anyway,' said Cassie.

'Never mind all that,' said Wen, 'how are you?'

'They aren't sure how well it will heal, but I'm alive.'

Cassie began a rundown of what had occurred as Wen made herself comfortable in a chair beside the bed and Jake propped himself up on a window ledge.

'So you think Brian Fletcher was the leader of this Priory organisation?' said Wen.

Cassie nodded. 'He's the teacher they talked about. It fits.'

After another ten minutes of conversation, the story was told. 'Is the Grand Master a patient here?' asked Wen.

'I'm presuming so,' said Cassie. 'To be honest, I've been preoccupied with other stuff.'

'I'd like to speak to him and this Mark Spencer,' said Wen, putting her head back and closing her eyes for a moment.

Cassie felt as if a weight had been lifted from her. She hadn't realised how alone she had felt until now, but she was part of a team again, and so grateful for that.

Wen almost fell asleep, but she had to be alert after Cassie's information, because she needed to talk to people, now.

Wen hadn't told Jake what she had read on the way down and she kept it from Cassie as well. She wasn't sure why, but she felt it was safer, to keep the knowledge to herself. Jake had forgotten all about Wen's comments, since all he was concerned with right now was recovering his stolen car.

'I need to make a few calls, Cassie,' said Wen. 'Could I borrow your phone, please?'

Cassie handed over her mobile and Wen went outside, leaving Cassie to console Jake.

Wen phoned her boss in Warrington. It was still very early, but she didn't care. 'Morning sir, I need your help.'

CHAPTER TWENTY-FIVE

Wen stood in front of the constable standing guard outside Leo Deeds room, who was glaring at her. 'Sorry, lady, but without ID you aren't going in.'

Wen stared back at him. 'It's ma'am to you, officer. If you call your chief, he'll tell you that I've had my ID stolen and I have the right to go in and talk to that man.'

He looked unsure, then turned away and pressed the button on his radio. 'Hello, Constable Browncroft here. Need verification for someone…' He walked away, and Wen could no longer hear the conversation.

It seemed an age before he turned back with a disgruntled look on his face. 'Sorry, ma'am. In you go.' He waved her in.

Wen smiled sweetly. 'Thank you, Officer,' she said as she opened the door.

'You need to leave the door open. And I'll be watching you, to be on the safe side.'

'Of course.' Wen was slightly annoyed at this, but if she had been in the same circumstances, she would have used due diligence. At least she knew her boss had done what she had asked, and contacted the Met to allow her to follow up her line of enquiry.

Leo Deed was lying in bed, swathed in bandages. He had a drip in his left arm, a tube in his nose and his eyes were shut. Wen felt as if she should tiptoe to his bedside, but as she actually wanted to speak to him, and had permission from the medical staff, there was little point in being unnaturally quiet. 'Mind you,' the consultant had warned, 'he's sedated and on pain meds, so I'm not sure what you'll get from him.'

She moved a chair closer to the bed and the harsh screech woke Leo. He looked at her through half-open eyes, still sleepy, then fumbled for his buzzer, terror on his face..

'Leo, it's OK. I'm Detective Chief Inspector Wen Price, from Cheshire. We spoke on the phone.'

His face scrunched up with concentration, then his features relaxed. 'DCI Price. Yes, now I remember,' he said hoarsely, then coughed. 'Sorry. My throat is sore from the tube they put in when I went to theatre.'

'And how are you now?'

'Tired, sore and feeling very old. How—' He coughed again. 'How is your officer?'

'She's doing OK.' Wen finally sat down. 'Leo, I need to ask you some questions, if you're up to it.'

He nodded and moved his head so he could see her better.

'Why did Brian Fletcher do that to you?'

'The poor man had lost his mind. Ranting about plots and conspiracy.' He tried to smile.

'I'm not having that, Leo. There are too many threads hanging loose right now. If I pull hard enough, I suspect I'll find a lead. One that you don't want me to have.'

Leo said nothing.

'All the things that have led up to this – you being in hospital, Cassie being almost murdered, your lackey Spencer killing Fletcher – all these things are linked, and you know what this is about.'

'Mark saved your officer's life, Wen. Don't forget that.'

'He did indeed, but what I want to know is why, after the first shot, he continued to fire. A full magazine went into that body. That's overkill, by anyone's standards.'

'He just… He lost control. He was shocked and thrown by what he had walked into. It must have been adrenaline.'

'Adrenaline?' Wen moved closer. 'And he always carries a gun, does he, just in case?'

Leo looked away and sighed. 'DCI Price, I had no idea about the gun. That is something you will have to ask Mark about, I'm afraid.'

'I intend to, believe me.'

'What has he said about the whole thing?' Leo enquired.

'Very little, just basic details. But he did say that Fletcher had probably attacked Truman Gryfinn. Do you know anything about that?'

Leo shook his head. 'Why would he do that?'

'What was Professor Gryfinn doing in London, Leo?' Wen's voice was quiet, but she couldn't keep an undertone of abruptness out of it.

'I've no idea. I'm his friend, not his keeper.' Leo rested his head back on his pillow, and Wen wondered how much longer she could press him for information.

'So, Leo, you think Mark Spencer acted the way he did because of shock and a surge of adrenaline?'

'Well, he must have been in a state of shock.'

At that, Wen stood up. 'Give me strength. His first shot hit Fletcher right in the centre of his forehead. That was a marksman's shot. What are you all hiding? People are being killed and injured for what? Some mythical scroll that could bring down the Christian world?'

For the first time, Leo looked shaken. 'What?'

'Isn't that what this is all about, Leo? You tell me. Is it all worth it? Brian Fletcher, for instance. The Teacher? The leader of the Priory? But I suppose you know nothing about that, either.'

'DCI Price, I don't know who told you that or where you heard it, but it is a myth. A conspiracy theory that does not hold water.'

'Actually, Leo, *you* told me. You said the Book of Sceleratis was the word of Christ, and I suspect you would think that was worth killing to protect.'

'You have misinterpreted me, DCI Price. I told you of the myth and how wonderful that would be, but if it ever was, it is now gone. We will never know. What we have witnessed is cruelty and violence which is terrible, but unrelated.'

Wen laughed, 'So, Leo, I'm supposed to believe that none of these things are linked.' Her voice rose. 'The man I loved had his head blown off, I almost died and my baby could have too, and all these murders have taken place to stop a possible artefact re-emerging.' She stood up. 'This stops *now*,' she shouted. 'And if I have to bring you and your church down to do it, I will.'

***

'Has he said anything more yet?' Wen asked Will Phillips, as he escorted her to the interview room at the police station where Mark Spencer was being held.

'He got around to asking for a solicitor eventually. The church has sent some big shot to represent him.'

'They do that. Close ranks.' Wen's mind went back to Bartholomew Fellows, who had also had a fancy brief sent by the church. He would have walked free if he hadn't attacked Cassie. Big mistake.

'Is the lawyer with him now?'

'Yep, all ready for you to talk to. Do you mind if I come in with you? Only my boss wants the credit for the arrest.' Phillips looked at Wen apologetically.

'No, that's fine. He's your force's collar, after all.'

They entered the interview room and sat opposite Mark Spencer and his brief, a smart man of about fifty, well-dressed and twitching with impatience. 'About time, may I say. We have been here for at least thirty minutes.'

'I'm sorry, Mr...' asked Wen

'Mateland,' he said, not making eye contact.

'Mr Mateland.' She smiled. 'You have been informed of your rights, Mr Spencer, so let's get on.' The recorder was switched on and everyone was named for the record.

'First of all,' said Mr Mateland, 'may I just say that I'm not happy with DCI Price being here. She is not from the Met and she was not involved with the arrest.'

'That is true,' said Wen, struggling to keep her composure. 'However, one of my officers was here at the Met's invitation. She was attacked during the incident where your client shot and killed the main suspect.'

'Even so—'

Spencer put his hand on his solicitor's arm. 'It's fine,' he said, his voice low and clear. 'What did you wish to ask?'

'Mr Spencer, I want to know why you had a gun with you, and why you not only shot the man, but filled him so full of holes that he could have been used as a colander?'

'The gun is mine and legally licensed. I have always held one since the last Grand Master had threats made against his life many years ago.' Spencer spoke without hesitation or expression.

'Do you carry it with you all the time?' asked Will Phillips.

'Not all the time. Usually when the Grand Master is in crowds: at big church events and such.'

'So, where were you when your boss was first attacked, and how did things get so out of hand?'

'I had been to visit Professor Gryfinn, but sadly he passed away before I could see him.'

'Why did you visit him?' asked Wen.

'At the Grand Master's request. He was most upset that his friend had been attacked and had ended up in hospital.'

'And when you got back…?' Wen prompted.

'I heard shouting from upstairs. I got my gun from my room and ran up. The rest you know.' He relaxed in his seat and examined the fingernails on his left hand.

'You don't seem very upset that you have taken a life, Mr Spencer,' said Wen.

'I look upon it as saving a life. Two, in fact. The Grand Master's, and that of your colleague. The man was completely out of his mind. There was no reasoning with him.'

'Have you ever killed before, Mr Spencer?' Wen linked her hands on the table.

'Don't answer that, Mark,' said Mateland.

'Never mind, I'm sure we can find out,' Wen remarked. 'But why discharge the whole magazine into him? That speaks of a lack of control to me.'

'I saved your officer's life, Detective Chief Inspector.' Now there was a hint of annoyance in Spencer's voice. 'And yes, I was angry. Perhaps, in the heat of the moment, I let my rage take over.'

'Have you heard of something called the Book of Sceleratis, Mr Spencer?'

Not a hint of recognition. 'No, never,' he said.

Wen decided to change tack. 'Going back to Professor Gryfinn, why was he here, in London?'

Mark shrugged. 'How should I know?'

'But you knew he had been admitted to hospital?'

'Yes. The ward staff asked if they could contact anyone for him, and he gave them the Grand Master's phone number.' Once again, he was in full control of himself.

'So, Brian Fletcher,' Wen continued. 'The Teacher.'

Mark frowned slightly. 'The who?'

'You didn't know he was The Priory's leader?'

Mark shook his head.

'And you don't know what The Priory are, what they stand for, what they are capable of?' Wen had a sinking feeling that Mark Spencer wouldn't admit to anything. He was well trained, and cool as a cucumber.

'Why didn't you talk to us sooner, Mark?' asked Will. 'And why did you wait to ask for legal representation?'

'He knew someone would be here as soon as possible,' said Mateland. 'And he also knew not to say too much until he had a solicitor present.'

'That wasn't much help, was it,' said Will Phillips, as they walked towards the main entrance of the station.

'No,' said Wen. 'All very well-rehearsed, if you ask me. What do you think he'll get in the end?'

'A couple of years, maybe, for manslaughter.'

'I agree. It was interesting that his brief cut him off when I asked if he'd ever killed anyone else.'

'Yes. Spencer was pretty calm about the whole thing. Will we find anything when we probe into his life, though?'

'Probably not. I was hoping that by speaking to him and his boss I might be able to get closer to closing the murder cases in our neck of the woods.'

'It's never that easy, though, is it?' Will pushed his hands into his pockets. 'Come on, I'll give you a lift back to the hospital.'

CHAPTER TWENTY-SIX

Wen walked into Cassie's room to find two sleeping members of her team. Cassie looked very comfortable, but Jake was sprawled across an armchair and would probably have a stiff neck when he woke.

Wen approached the bed and Cassie opened her eyes. 'Sorry,' murmured Wen as she took the seat closest to her colleague. 'I didn't mean to wake you.'

'You didn't, not really. I had my eyes closed but I wasn't asleep, unlike Jake.' She nodded at the inert body. 'He hasn't shut up about his bloody car,' she whispered. 'He says it was stolen to order, and by now it's probably in a shipping container, heading to Russia. I pretended to be asleep to stop him wittering.' She said it with a smile, but Wen knew what she meant. She had gone through the same when they were waiting for the police at Watford Gap.

Cassie tried to push herself into a sitting position, grimacing with pain.

'Here, let me help you.' Wen tried to support Cassie's injured arm as she got into a comfortable position. She almost fell back into her chair, beginning to feel her lack of sleep.

'How did you get on?' Cassie asked, as she relaxed into her pillows.

'I got exactly nowhere.' Wen rubbed her tired eyes, blinked and sat back. 'Leo is sticking with the line that it's all a conspiracy and there's no truth in the book, which probably did exist but doesn't now. And Mark Spencer, who is now all lawyered up, was surprisingly talkative.'

Cassie looked hopefully at Wen. 'About what?'

'About why he had a gun and why he got carried away shooting Brian Fletcher. He had a reasonable explanation, and I don't think we could shake his resolve even if we had more evidence, which we don't.'

'But he did save my life, Wen, and Fletcher did have a manic look on his face when he attacked me.'

'Do you think we're looking for something that isn't there, Cassie?'

'I don't think we'll ever know: whoever's been behind this has covered their tracks so well. I don't think we should stop looking, but…'

'But we may not get the answers we want. And I hate it. It's like a wound that's trying to scab over, and when I pick at it I get nowhere…' Wen put her head in her hands.

'Wen, you need to step away from this,' said Cassie. 'The squad needs you. God knows when I'll be back to full health, though I suppose I can do office work even with a bad arm.'

Wen smiled. 'First things first. Let me sort out your transfer to a local hospital.' She looked at Jake, still asleep. 'I need to get back to Warrington later today, and I want you where I can come and see you whenever I can – or whenever you need me.'

***

Three weeks later, Wen sat at her desk and went through all the paperwork on local unresolved murders. The inquiry in Malta had been scaled down considerably, and she had promised Luca a call in a few weeks to tie up loose ends.

Loose ends? Who was she kidding. It was as if a kitten had been playing with a ball of wool and wrapped it around all the furniture, twice.

Her chief had told her, in no uncertain terms, not to spend much more time on the case.

'But four unsolved murders, sir.'

'Two on our patch, DCI Price,' he corrected. 'The other is Liverpool's, not ours, and the fourth isn't even in our country.'

Wen bit her lip to stop her from saying something she knew

she would regret later.

'Look, Wen, I know this is personal for you, and not easy to let go of, but we need to move forward. *You* need to move forward. We have no leads, no forensics, no suspects.'

'Yes, but—'

'Yes but nothing. DI Rowden's back next week?'

'Yes, sir.'

'And DS Briggs?'

'Back at the end of the month, sir. We're unsure about DC Wall. She's still having treatment.'

'Right. I believe you're going to job-share with DI Rowden until she is completely recovered. And that will enable you to have the rest of the leave you're entitled to? '

'Yes, sir.'

'Excellent.' He dismissed her as he always did, by opening a file on his desk.

Wen felt as if she had left the job half finished, and it didn't sit well with her. The only person who was going to court within the whole story was Mark Spencer, and his defence were claiming PTSD. Apparently, he had served with Special Ops in Afghanistan, seeing and doing things that no one should have to. His service record had been largely redacted, and wasn't worth looking at. He would probably get a suspended sentence, with a stipulation that he attend therapy.

Leo was at his villa in Spain, recovering. He wasn't prepared to talk to Wen at this point in time, and probably not at any time in the future.

Wen was pushing papers around her desk, notes of her own making which she knew almost verbatim, when her phone rang.

'Hi,' said Cassie. 'How's tricks?'

'Oh, you know. I've just been warned not to spend too much time on our case, but I was expecting that.'

'And will you?'

'I'll still look for leads in my own time. I'm not giving up, Cassie.'

'I never thought you would.'

'Yes, well, let's park that for now. How are you, and are you ready for work on Monday?'

'Good, and yes.' Cassie had been allowed to return to light duties, and the force had even allocated her a driver.

'I'll be here Monday morning to hand over to you, then I'm off for a few days. My daughter has forgotten what I look like.'

'Ah, but she has Rose.'

'Yes, thank God for Rose. I fell on my feet when I employed her.'

'You had to have some lucky breaks, Wen. Anything interesting come in for us lately?'

'Some human remains have been found at Grappenhall, but they could be ancient. John's there now.' Wen could visualize Cassie rubbing her hands together, in anticipation of a good old murder to investigate.

'Right, lovely. I'll see you on Monday.'

***

Wen was pleased to get home that night knowing that Daisy would be fed and ready for bed and there would be bean chilli for supper. It was Wednesday, and Aran always made bean chilli on a Wednesday.

As she hung her coat on the newel post, she could hear Aran explaining the best way to cook rice. Rose, bless her, actually sounded interested. But maybe she was. All Wen knew was that Rose and Aran got on very well: another little miracle.

'Hi, you two,' Wen called.

'Hello,' they replied, in unison.

Rose came into the hall and collected her coat and bag, ready to set off for home.

'Daisy been good for you?' Wen enquired.

'As gold. She has her check-up next Tuesday; do you want me to take her?'

'I should be free, Rose, but you can come as well if you like.'

Rose smiled happily. 'Yes, please.' She headed for the door, then stopped. 'Oh, almost forgot. The dry cleaning I picked up for you?'

'Yes,' said Wen, wondering which of her favourite garments they had ruined this time.

'They found this in the lining of your jacket pocket.' Rose delved in her bag and pulled out a small object. Wen opened her hand, palm up to receive the item, and Rose dropped a pen drive onto it.

The End

THE WARRINGTON DETECTIVE

For I Have Sinned.
Chapter one

The Reverend Mathew Coburn was kneeling at the altar of his church, deep in prayer. He was praying for forgiveness, for guidance. What he had been told in the confessional was sacred, he could not repeat those words, to anyone. But such evil. He should, no, he must go to the police, he had no choice. He had to protect those still alive. So intense was his meditative state, he was not aware of the person now standing directly behind him, until it was too late.

***

John Barron got to the burial site early. He was three days into an exhumation of human remains in the village of Grappenhall, and what he and his team had uncovered could be explained by the place they had been found.

John knew that he should have left this to others, that his backlog of work needing his expertise was more urgent, but a day or two would not make that much difference. His customers cannot go anywhere.

It was so good to get out of the morgue and do some field work for a change. Tomorrow a forensic anthropologist, Doctor Emily Hanson, was joining them with her high-tech equipment, and once she arrived, John knew he would definitely be back in his office.

The find had been due to a new wall being erected around the perimeter of St Saviors church, the previous wooden one had rotted and had got to the stage where it was dangerous

To find unmarked graves at the edge of the local cemetery, like these, were common. Here the disavowed were placed, people who died in work houses, unmarried mothers, often with their dead babies, deaths of prisoners. Basically, people that had not led righteous lives, according to the law of the land, at the time of their deaths.

So far, they had collected bones of seven humans, but it had been the last set of remains that had been interesting, this was what had caused the forensic team to say, 'hang on a minute, that's not right.' Not as old as the others, in fact this body had a tooth filling that had probably been done about twenty years ago. This looked more like a dump site to John, and he now had that corpse back at his morgue, but he wanted to look a bit further today, before he left the rest of the work to his team and Dr Hanson.

He was just putting on his protective gear when he noticed the church door was wide open. It was usually locked up at this time of day, and this inconsistency alarmed John. He slipped his arms into his forensic suit and as he zipped it up, he started to walk towards the open door.

It was dark inside, and he had to adjust his eyes from the light outside on this late summer's day, to the shrouded greyness of the church's interior. He stopped in his tracks. There was blood, a lot of blood. John unzipped his over suit and fished out his phone from his shirt pocket. He found the number he wanted and pressed call.

'Hello Cassie. Its John Barron here. I'm at St Saviors. Yes, Grappenhall Village. Sorry to disturb you so early, but there is something here I think you should see.'

***

Linsey tried to open her eyes, but found it both difficult and painful. She was almost sure her nose was broken, but if you have your face slammed against a wall with some force, that would often be the outcome.

She wanted to get up, which she could, just about in her cage, but he had told her not to move, not a muscle, so she was going to stay exactly in this spot for as long as she could. How long would that be? How long had she been here? The light was on continually, there were no windows and Linsey had lost track of the hours, the days, because time didn't exist here. Only pain, fear, and dread.

When would she be missed? Not for weeks. She had taken a long overdue holiday on her own to walk in the Lake District. No fixed plans, just go where the path took her. She began to giggle; this place wasn't going to get many recommendations on trip advisor. The giggles turned into sobs, deep and uncontrolled.

What was it he had said when she screamed, 'people will be looking for me.'

'Not yet they won't, and when they do, it will be too late.'

MORE BY THE SAME AUTHOR

All Manor of People

I'll never be a Ninja Now

Just a little Prick

**The Warrington detective 1
Searching for Evil**

**The Warrington Detective 2
The Vien Killer**

Millions of little Pricks

All available on Amazon.co.uk

Printed in Great Britain
by Amazon